About the Author

Mike Brennen grew up in the Bahamas, and moved to the United States as an adult, first as a college student, then to settle in a career as a chemist. He has always had a passion for storytelling. Also, as a man of faith, he is a leader in the Methodist church. His wife is Barbara. They have six children and eleven grandchildren. They live in Delray Beach, Florida.

Eastern God, Western Winds

Mike Brennen

Eastern Gods, Western Winds

Olympia Publishers
London

www.olympiapublishers.com
OLYMPIA PAPERBACK EDITION

Copyright © Mike Brennen 2023

The right of Mike Brennen to be identified as author of
this work has been asserted in accordance with sections 77 and 78 of
the Copyright, Designs and Patents Act 1988.

All Rights Reserved

No reproduction, copy or transmission of this publication
may be made without written permission.
No paragraph of this publication may be reproduced,
copied or transmitted save with the written permission of the publisher,
or in accordance with the provisions
of the Copyright Act 1956 (as amended).

Any person who commits any unauthorized act in relation to
this publication may be liable to criminal
prosecution and civil claims for damage.

A CIP catalogue record for this title is
available from the British Library.

ISBN: 978-1-80439-309-3

This is a work of fiction.
Names, characters, places and incidents originate from the writer's
imagination. Any resemblance to actual persons, living or dead, is
purely coincidental.

First Published in 2023

Olympia Publishers
Tallis House
2 Tallis Street
London
EC4Y 0AB

Printed in Great Britain

Dedication

Dedicated to my parents, Audley and Anna Brennen, who told me their stories, which shaped my experiences as I watched them survive numerous obstacles with few complaints.

Acknowledgments

Thanks to my extended community in Florida and the Bahamas that allowed me to find a home, where I felt at home. I wanted to write about them, so I did. Finally, I am extremely grateful to my wife, Barbara, and to our children, who are always honest and kindly supportive of my projects.

Prologue

Even when Christ walked on earth in the east, griots from Africa (back then it was known as Ethiopia) crossed the ocean to the west. Terrific winds blew their hand-hewn ships to the "Land of the Great Spirit." They lived and loved with the westerners, later to be called Indians. These Ethiopian griots knew of the sadness and gladness of the straight hair, red-skinned peoples of the land, later to be called America. When they returned to Ethiopia they made legend with charming stories of this remarkable continent beyond the Great Sea.

The people who worshiped a God they called "Great Spirit" had their own version of storytellers. They tell us of shrines built to honor their majestic dark-skinned visitors. The worlds of the west and of the east grew toward each other for centuries. The songs and tales carried back and forth along the equatorial winds of the Atlantic Ocean.

More than a thousand years went by after Christ returned to heaven. A new society of the east grew in numbers and knowledge. They developed in the continent of Europe. And they too learned of the great continent beyond the ocean through their navigators like the ones called Columbus and Vespucci.

They too came to this "Land of the Great Spirit." But they came like conspirators in the night, planting flags, staking lands, and seeking gold. Thus, they could not live and love with the western peoples because conspiracies destroy the foundation of friendship. But their voyages have also become legend.

Now each of the people who came has a story. The red-skinned ancestors of those ancient Americans still mourn to the slow rhythm of drums, singing their regrets as to how their beloved lands were lost. The pale-skin ancestors of the ancient Europeans, on the other hand, still enjoy the moving pictures, called "Westerns," that show, in magnificent color, how their prized West was won. And the dark-skinned ancestors of the ancient Africans still stretch out their hands and wait wantonly to rule the earth again, which some believe will happen just before Christ returns to again walk on earth.

Time keeps moving on. As is written and told, the European conspiracy to win the west was realized. Again, they conspired to win the world, and the world was won.

Now these custodians of history – African griots, story tellers of the so-called Indians, and the Europeans who make moving pictures – will join in a newer world. This is a world where east meets west, but many of us don't know east from west.

Homeless

It was bitter London cold, and his scanty-soled boots scraped sidewalk snow. They called him "Black Hobo," but his name was what he called himself.

He was thinking the king had died – King George's funeral – a state occasion. He was visualizing the series of religious processions and coffin-pretty speeches. Later, he would imagine and explain the circumstance of the pomp to Betsy.

She alone listened and thought so much of him. He could recite all the kings and queens, beginning from William the Conqueror. Because he was not from England she was even more impressed. She was white, English, and almost illiterate. He was Black, from the colonies, and took it for granted to know, because he was drilled with Royal Reader exercises since his starched cotton shirt preparatory school days.

She, completely homeless, had a past that remained a mystery. And though he knew history, he too had a past mystery. The pages he opened for her were only superfluous and diverting subplots.

An expanse of ocean and an elapse of years had obscured the dark storms, which had blown him to cloudy England. The drizzled wet coat and his droopy posture contrasted with those starched shirts of his youth, yet he still showed sharpened faculties. He wished for another layer of clothes.

He approached Downing Street. He walked around a snorting horse, harnessed to a carriage, with no riders. However, many riders and carriages would be coming soon. The king had died, and there was going to be a grand funeral in England.

Book 1

Brad

Bridges

Lake Okeechobee is covered with algae because sugar water from the farm factories makes it eutrophic – too much fertilizer, too much algae. The lake is unseen and separated by weeds and palmettos and pines and mosquitoes. It is far away. The sun is fading, yet it peeps through tall pine trees and above water hyacinths, because it is still brilliant. Florida's forest, if Florida can claim a forest, is still illuminated. In its weedy crevice, in a dirt pathway is an unusual shadow.

Twilight approaches. Clouds sandwich the sun like the insides of fresh-baked bread and red herring. Wind rustles the pine. Needle leaves drop on the metal roof. Breezes cool the evening woods. A gleam of sunlight flashes in the rear-view mirror of a blue Plymouth sedan. The car is out of place and pace – eventide interrupted – for even the crows have folded their wings in final prayer as dark tranquility creeps.

The sedan bounces furiously. Long toes with polished nails curl and grasp the window glass of the opened rear door. Squat toes grip sandy soil, another set sticks into space. Legs tense. Lean and soft embrace broad and hard muscles. Both sets glisten with sweat from great effort. Guttural screams disturb the silence. Darkness is still to come.

Currents of wind are attracted to enmeshed bodies in the back seat. Breezes cool the male's back, but he notices nothing. The sun is alive in the slight breeze. The forest claims all for itself. The "Great Spirit," caretaker of these woods, breathes out the wind, and the sleepy vision of the "Spirit" is red like setting sun.

Mists of sweat mingle with fragrance, escape; it smells like perspiration, perfume and pine. The Florida backfield is permeated with a never-before, and never-again, essence – spirit like. The male body stiffens. The red toes of the woman follow her curling legs. She embraces and pulls the firm folds of his behind toward her vortex of creation.

He groans. She screams. The herring sun slips from the sandwich of clouds. The dirt road darkens. Man and woman cling to each other, aware of only loud breathing and quickened heartbeats.

The night again belongs to the natives. A tiny squirrel scoots down a tree and disappears into the darkness. The owl hoots into the silence, and a cricket sends his plaintive cry into the night. The Plymouth withdraws slowly from the scene, leaving a pollution of carbon monoxide smoke and tire trails, earthquake to a nest of red ants.

When Brad dropped Bet back to her West Palm Beach house, the waning half-moon glimmered. He left without daring to come inside. She waved bye; he drove on toward Miami.

The door closed silently and sneakily on her behind. On the outside, an artificial Christmas wreath, electric candle blinking in the middle, hung to a nail. It was New Year's Day evening. She was nineteen years old and full of promise.

She went straight to her room and sprawled on the flowery bedspread. Maybe she did not kiss a goodnight peck because he was still with her – in her. Yet she would not see him again. Tomorrow, she would get in back of the Trailways bus to Daytona. Christmas vacation was over. She did not think too much about anything. She just rolled her lankiness onto the bed and wrinkled the flowery bed cover.

Papa Rolle, in the back room, fiddled with the phonograph you didn't have to crank, a Christmas present to the family – but, really, to himself. The record played *Auld Lang Syne*. The diamond needle found its grooves, the choir sang. His daughter listened, and without knowing, or caring, tears escaped onto a bothersome embroidered sheet.

Inside of Bet, something moves. The New Year's hymn floats into the night – into the Spirit. Creation listens. Songs of rejuvenation pay tribute to tradition. New life seeks recent death, which seeks old life. The annual cry of uncounted souls bridges the entire race. This night, melancholy souls gaze at a half-moon reflection of the sun, in a star-glittered sky, each star a sun in its own galaxy. Life reaches for more life.

She hears music from an inner listening ear. The female alto brings Auld Lang Syne to a climax, and the choir of mixed voices brings it to a close. Static repeats itself, the needle scratches empty grooves. The squeak of Papa's chair opens her outer ear – and she is now aware of heaving in her lungs, the sound that separates inner from outer ear.

Bet let her tears flow like a gentle rain on a hot day. Like a mystic on a carpet, she arose from the bed. Now she could smell the black-eyed peas. She notices the ruffling curtain against her opened bedroom window and feels the cool wetness against her cheekbones. Brad was far from her; he had gone into the night.

Brad drove south along the Dixie. He was not thinking of the other woman now, nor did he really think of the present one. Instead his mind was at peace. Someone was praying for him.

His mother – an Inagua woman – told him that, "This is the

peace from above," she said. "People can pray so deep for you, your mind would just go rest awhile."

They would sit on the cold stone kitchen floor. His daddy, captain of the mail boat, would be gone – sometimes over a week. Then it would be just them two – him and his Ma, and no Pa.

But, in fact, right now, if Brad could see past the ocean horizon, he would see some cumbersome diesel boat chugging through slightly choppy waves, ten feet above the coral rock. Right now, his Pa, just like him, is a nighttime traveler. Across the waters, Captain Collins peers ahead, as he handles the huge steering wheel. However, he knows where the boat is going without seeing. He has done this trip so many nights.

Both son and father meander their vehicles through a comfortable night. Each glance at the gleaming moon in the sky. The water vessel wakes the resting waters, which gushes and ripples into a nothingness that would not reach the nearest land. The car engine rumbles, the Plymouth alone on the highway with its lone driver, trudging toward the city. Night crickets wail, like a refrain, pleading with the wind to carry their song out to sea.

Brown Skin Gal

She had the smoothest and clearest skin – like the Indians. No, not the Indians and Cowboys. The Indians Columbus couldn't find? No, not them – and not the West Indians, either. In fact, she had no kind of Indian in her, because she is a Bahamian. And that is that. But, boy, she had some smooth skin!

She was the one he met at the dock after his Pa fired him off the mail boat. He remembered her – she was the one who kissed him on the "Rocky Road," which was planned to one day pave new residential developments in Nassau. Children should know to come straight home from school, but some of them stopped to "spin the bottle." The kiss was sudden and brazen. Yep, how could he forget.

The fisherman in the docked dinghy already had her four-shilling note for the fish she was buying. The man in the boat scraped rough scales from a Grunt Snapper.

Brad was just back from Inagua, working on his daddy's mail boat, delivering groceries and mail to that remote southern Out Island. That was not what he wanted to do after finishing school, but that was what he had to do. But, he could not take the stress and cussing from Captain Collins, his daddy.

"You think you entitled," he heard the British Guiana man yell. "Well no one ever entitled me – I had to carry my weight. You better clean out that hole. As long as you work on this boat, you do as you are instructed. Or get the hell off."

Brad got the hell off.

Now here she comes, (what was her name?) from the other side of the hill, come to buy fish. She leaned into the dinghy to get her grunts; her bosom leaned against the frail fabric of dress. She had matured from womanish to woman. He watched.

"You buy enough for me?" he teased.

"Well, I'll be—you ask me for fish, and you work on a boat. You shoulda bring me some." She showed even white teeth. She strung the straw through the mouth of about a half-dozen cleaned fish, looped the rest of straw around her middle fingers, prepared to walk home with a string of fish.

"I just quit the boat." That came out involuntarily. He saw again the angry image of the man everybody called Captain Collins, never by another name. He pushed back the image, and also the tear that rose like a flowing tide.

"How could you quit, and your daddy is the captain?" she asked, sort of, as she walked away from the dockside. She glanced behind, as if expecting him to follow.

He hopped ahead to reach her side. "You still livin' on East Street?"

"Chile, daddy ain't goin' nowhere. He could buy some land real cheap on the other side of Wulff Road, where they pushin' the trail back south. But he say he born on East Street, and that's where he ga' die."

"But if he go south, it will still be East Street. It will be East Street south."

"Yeah – that don't mean the same for him. He born on the real East Street." She poked his side and winked with a playful accusation. "You know what I mean, Bradford Collins."

He followed the twinkle in her eye, the challenge – and invitation – for sweet casual talk. "Well, I guess I'll have to come and move you out of old East Street."

"You trying to propose?" She laughed. "You better quit jiving. How many women you have? Probably one in every island."

"Do you want to go to the cinema on Saturday?" Just like that he asked her to go to the show – well, well.

Her plump behind pushed ahead as they climbed to the top of East Street Hill. This was part of the ridge that ran the northern coast of the island. Town was on the north side of the hill – Bay Street; and on the south side was where colored folks lived – over the hill. At the top of the hill, she looked back and smiled on him. Then she leaned back to walk down the hill.

He gazed at the firm in her calf muscles. Then he glanced up at a tree full of guineps. He jumped sudden and grabbed a bunch. Couple fell on the hot asphalt road. Biting into the skin of one, still on the bunch, he tasted the gelatin coating of the inside seed. Yep, these were sweet. He broke off a few for him and gave the bunch to her hand that had no fish.

"How you ga' take me to the show when you out of a job? Remember, you just quit the boat."

"That ain't your business, girl. You just get ready. Here, these some sweet guineps. They sweet like me."

Now that he was walking even with her, he noticed that perspiration dampened the underarm of her dress. Her teeth were so white, framed by such brown skin, as she bit into the green skin of the stolen fruit.

"You tief these people guineps, an' put me in partner with you." She laughed. "I hope you don't tief no money to take me to the show. You done make me a receiver."

"I gat money, girl. I don't steal." He thought, Mama would give me money.

The marquee of the movies loomed ahead – "Now

Showing." As they slowed, he stared at Clark Gable leaning into the remarkable lipstickedy face of a lovely actress, whatever was her name. Just below his moustache, her mane of golden hair seemed to sway in a breeze. The smell of buttered popcorn wafted in the air.

"Well, I want to sit in the balcony, Bradford. Are you goin' to buy balcony seats?"

"Sure, baby," said Brad.

That girl was Petunia, who was to become the other woman. That was the one he took to the cinema. Then he took her back to her house, but he did not take her inside. He took her outside, in the outhouse, while the door was locked from inside. That is how it started with that Petunia girl.

Week after week, he took her to the show, and in the outside toilet. And they thought nobody noticed. They was doin' it so slick and quick. He acted like he had to go to the toilet, then she would sneak around back, and he would let her inside when no one was in sight. They never took off any clothes – they were so quick – because it was just a li'l bit.

But every little bit hurts. It was not too long, one Saturday night, when she ran from her seat to the inside toilet of the theater. She heaved and threw up, and she knew something was wrong. They left before the end of the show.

Walking home, she told him, "You know, I missed my time of the month."

They passed a forest of bushes and trees, a vacant lot, which was a landmark for the side road that led to her Papa's house.

"What you trying to say, Petunia?"

"That my time is not comin'. Don't you know what that means?" Her nose flared.

"I know what you mean. I'm not stupid." His mother had

just explained what it meant a few weeks ago. Before then, he really never knew. Of course women got pregnant from grinding sex, and they had babies. No big bird brought a baby. The women got big and bigger, then the midwife came, and there was the new baby. He knew the open and casual talk of the men, but not the closed chatter of womanly concerns. So, in his best male voice, he asked, "Are you sure you big, girl?"

"Listen, Brad, I know you is a man, and don't understand these things, but I never miss. I am regular." She laughed, but it came from her outer throat. She was not amused.

"What you planning to do?" His voice too echoed from a hollow place.

They had reached the banister of the outside porch. She held onto it and sat herself on the porch steps. She hung her head. He could not hear the sound she made, so he asked her to say it again.

She raised the pitch of her voice. "I said, Papa will kill me for sure. He already treat me like some outside child – and he so mean when he get to drinking."

"He not ga' kill you. You his flesh and blood."

"Well you know, Mama found out about us – you know. She say, if I get pregnant, I better learn how to take care of the baby. Say she gotta work and can't raise no before-time children."

"Well you need to go to the nurse, because you don't know for sure."

"Everyone will be calling me "Dyna," a hot and loose woman. My name will be gone."

"Well if you expectin', you expectin'." Brad had pushed a piece of straw from a coconut palm leaf between his teeth where the cinema popcorn got stuck. "As long as the baby is mine, I will support it."

She whirled back at him. She heaved but repressed the

nausea. She sucked in her breath and her snot. She was silently crying, but she got right close to his face.

"What the frig you mean by that?" she asked. Then, without waiting for an answer: "What you mean if it is yours? Who else own you think it would be? Just because I live on East Street, and we don't have much money like your family, you think I'm bad. Well you the only who could be the daddy, cause you the only one I gone with. And I thought you was different and decent. Boy, I shoulda listen to what Mama tell me – now, I ga have to raise a child by myself. And Papa done told me he'll kill me if I go get pregnant, 'doin' all that freshness with you." Her body leaned and resigned into the porch banister.

"Listen here, I said I'll take care of the baby – if you really having a baby. I know how to get a job. I just want to be sure you ain't trying to put me in no trick." As he spoke, his eyes caught a movement in the twilight.

This middle-aged woman entered the yard with a straw basket, heavy with Saturday groceries balanced on her head. This was Petunia's mother who approached the porch.

She was gazing at her daughter. The daughter lifted her head and gazed back. Brad noticed the shiny sweat on her forehead, and the focus of her eyes. He felt and watched the mother quicken her steps.

"What's wrong with you girl? What you cryin' for?"

Brad answered, even though he was not spoken to, "She's pregnant." Then he picked at his teeth with the piece of straw.

The older woman looked at him. He saw a distance and reproach in her eyes. Then he remembered what he had overheard her say one time – "His Ma is the Inagua woman who took up with that foreign boat captain. You know she left her husband for him, left him in Inagua. Now she in Nassau, livin' with him; she think she such a big shot, but she jus' a salty foot gal, no better than the rest of us."

Now he felt all the trouble in the wall had hurdled – the wall he hid behind. This was his first glance into those eyes, eyes that he did not know had X-ray vision, and they had examined his every move when he was not looking. Now, without expression, they gazed in his direction.

The voice also carried no emotion. "I know she's pregnant." Then she fully faced her daughter.

In back of Petunia's house, this rich white man had built this giant wall. It separated the poor from the rich, the colored from the white. Brad felt a separation like that – and he was the poor one. The huge wall was the shoulder of Petunia's mother that reached out to embrace her child. It was as forbidding as the back of this woman's graying head.

Once, for fun, he had jumped the white man's wall. He landed on the other side and wanted to stay. He did not, could not. He stole an orange from one of the trees, then leaped the giant stone-wall and barbed-wires back into the weedy bushes of Petunia's yard. In her yard, he thought, "I don't belong here, but I'm supposed to be here."

Now he was on the wrong side of a shoulder, cold to him, but warmly embracing her child. He thought, out of the blue, "I'm supposed to be holdin' the mother of my first child."

This is rest of the story with Petunia. Her Papa never did put her out, never tried to whip her, none of that foolishness. The mother would have left his drunken behind. She told him so and meant every word. *After all she went through for that girl, you all just don't know.*

The daughter, expecting her child, did move out anyway. She went to her Grandma to live. But just before the baby was due, she moved back home. Her belly was big and taut like a heated goat-skin Junkanoo drum, and her nose was twin bugles.

They had stopped going to the show. They had their own reality. Sometimes he visited the grandma's house, sat in the old women's yard under the dilly tree, on an old upside washing tub. He was learning the mechanic trade, working odd jobs, making a few shillings here and there. When he didn't work he stopped by to visit.

On a cool February night the baby came. Petunia, was back at her mother's house when the pain hit. The younger brother was sent racing to the midwife. The nurse came quickly, chased out the males, washed her hands in Dettol solution, boiled water and delivered from the girl turned woman (despite her screaming and thrashing) a healthy baby girl. The scale that the nurse bought showed eight-pound, five ounces.

Brad came the next day. He was there all day. Everyone in the British colony had a day off for mourning – the King of England was getting buried. They let Brad hold the baby, his baby. He watched the children play – no school. They played rounders. One child knocked the spongy red ball way over the giant wall; the other scaled the wall to retrieve the ball.

The mother screamed, "Get down from that wall before you break your neck."

Brad laughed. "That's little children," he thought. "They always want to jump a fence."

Petunia's mother even smiled his way, her teeth opened. Great God Almighty! She offered him a white and red-trimmed enameled plate chock full of peas and rice and fried fish, with a tablespoon stuck under the mound of rice. He ate on the front porch. He felt at home.

When the baby got big enough to eat food, the young parents, they moved into a rented clapboard house. Though no crazy Papa made Bradford marry Petunia, the new family followed the common law. The landlord was a lawyer, a friend of Mr. Collins, Brad's father. Here they were in a new world, soon to get married, but they never did. They just lived together with the baby girl in their shack of a home.

Their world extended from the south side of Wulff Road, on the new part of East Street, north, to the sea docks, in town. When they moved it was summer in Nassau, but the way time flies, winter would soon come, and by New Year the baby would walk.

Bradford Collins became a stevedore – three pound and ten shillings each week. He always could find a job – and he was never lazy to work. That was one thing even Petunia's mother admitted about him.

Their new world was surrounded by a bigger planet. Their world was a tiny concentric, but one with widening circles. The Great War was finished. Clouds of radioactive dust settled over Japan. Allied forces looked toward a new sunshine, as the dark menace of Germany was dismantled into a divided country. Yet Britain became weary, even though the darling Elizabeth would be coronated Queen Elizabeth II. And all of Europe, as if they had run out of effort, to the United States, they relayed the power baton to lead the human race to a new world order.

The waterways of the world became ocean routes for leisure travel again. Those fortunate ones from the temperate zone escaped gray winter snow, and jumped on the hotel-sized cruise ships, destined for the tropic sun. It was good to play again; it was time to settle your nerves, because the war had unsettled everyone.

The new routes converged onto Brad and Petunia's island

home, into Nassau Harbour. The young couple found hope. They too had been thrust into the war of life, and now found hope in peacetime. Maybe these sunshine lovers would bring money. Brad spoke excitement everyday with gleaming eyes and blustering speech. He unloaded the boats and watched them unload those sunshine seekers who flashed Yankee dollars at wide-eyed natives.

But his excitement waned. First he heard the rumor. A week later he learned it was true – the shipping company was laying off stevedores as the shipping season slowed. The name Bradford Collins was scribbled on the list circulated by the foreman. The next day they sent him home. His little baby girl – Georgia – had grown two conspicuous front teeth and was just learning to walk.

"Maybe I can work construction at one of the new hotels they starting to build out west." His thoughts came to a dead hush, before hoping out loud.

"How come they cut you loose?" Petunia asked. "I thought your uncle was the foreman. What kind of family you got?" She rocked the baby, without looking at him.

"Not 'cut loose' girl, laid off, just for a while. Don't you know the difference between 'cut loose' and 'laid off'? They'll call us back when the winter season come, and when the hotel business pick up again."

She raised herself up, and rested the sleeping child on the bed, crossways. "You the one don't know the difference – because they the same. They goin' pay you while you 'laid off', huh?"

He gave no answer to this sensible young woman. She was right, but he had hope. He expected his final three pound-ten shillings envelope.

She was right too, about saving, then their future would not rest on his final pay. He did never open that Post Office account. When she had told him, he said he was the man. He gave her one pound-ten shillings every week. He kept two pounds to throw away on Haitian liquor at the Last Chance bar, next to the dock.

He was wrong to drown his future in the bottle, and she tried to make it right. One time, on his payday, she showed up at the bar with the baby on her hip. That shamed him. That was the first time he slapped her down, not wanting to but liquor and male friends influenced his unexpected violent abuse, because it was expected that women stay in their place.

"Don't try that mess with me girl," he cried. The half-empty glass was in his hand.

He was wrong too about hitting her, just because she was right. And being the man and hitting her did not make him right. That is why he said nothing when he realized that 'cut loose' and 'laid off' was the same. He just stayed silent and thought about his fate, an old rum bottle, plugged tight, full of mistakes and empty with good times, gone, drifting without direction, beyond the Nassau dock. He looked at her smooth wet forehead, her pretty brown skin. Then he looked down at the raised bronzed veins of her hands, as she shook out a big towel to cover the baby. He thought to himself, "While I was gone, loading those ships, she has stayed home and minded this baby, all by herself."

Outside Mother

Oh Lord, I hollered to my Maker. What is this generation coming to – these now-a-day children do more foolishness than the law allow.

Look what that Bradford boy done gone and do to my baby child. I should have been a man. Back in my day, any daddy what worth his name would have him and her before the preacher before God could wink.

But that no accounting husband of mine must be afraid; but no, he ain't afraid of nobody, and if you give him a couple of drinks, he'll speak his sober mind. It's something else that doesn't make him stand up for Petunia. And I know, I really shouldn't fault him. Really I have to take the full blow for whatever happens to her, my first baby child.

Sometimes, Lord, I think, it ain't fair what pain a woman gets to bear. You know, 'specially when men like Bradford plant their seed and try to take off like a hound dog. But look like Brad not running – his parents must be shame. At least they making him support her and the baby – even though I never hear 'bout any proposal.

I still can't stand that boy's mother. She thinks she is Mistress It, but she just a salty foot Inagua girl who left her husband to take up with that foreign boat captain. She knows he supposed to marry Petunia, but she think her boy too good for my girl.

But I didn't get no better when I was pregnant with Petunia. At least Petunia still get to see Brad, and he still help. I got it worse, because I never seen Petunia daddy since that sunny day I got hot in Whale Cay.

Before Bertram came into my story and married me and saved my reputation, there was a boy from Bimini. Nobody knows about him except me and you, Lord. I would have followed him to the top of the hill and to the bottom of the ocean. He never asked all of that. But I did what he asked. And I sneaked and prayed that not one single solitary could ever discover what happened. His name never came out of my breath to nobody since that day.

Back in those tough days my aunt got me a job on Whale Cay. This rich woman owned the island and made it like a resort for other wealthy folks to vacation. That was a good woman. She hired a bunch of Bahamians to upkeep the place. People came from all over to get hired. My parents sent me to Auntie who got me a job in the laundry room. That is how I met that boy, bringing his dirty clothes and underwear to wash.

"I don't know if these yellow stains on your drawers will come out unless they are bleached. Then the bleach will fade the underpants." My poor self was greener than new grass.

He laughed in a deep cackled bass. "Girl, you don't know what's that stain?" Under his slight moustache were thinnish lips, opened to show a gold-capped tooth.

Next thing that boy is causing me to sweat with all kinds of fresh talk – about wet dreams and masturbations – conversations to which my body instantly warmed and to which my curiosity piqued. Then, he is telling me about how to do it and, hintingly, asking me to do it. He is grinning with that glamorous gold tooth, and I am laughing in the womanish way that my Ma or Aunty would not approve. Anyone of them would fetch me a blow, which would quell any hormonal rush.

The motorboat belonged to the American who came to fish for fun, but my boy worked for this man. And he could run it when the man was not on the island. "Have you ever gone on a motorboat ride?"

I say, "No."

"Do you want to go tomorrow?"

I hear myself, "Yes." Lord, you know Auntie woulda kill me with a beating if she ever found out what happened the next day. But it happened.

My womanhood exploded on the boat. It hurt, the blood shamed me, but he had somehow learned to be gentle. This was a jokey guy, and he cracked one after the other while the boat was anchored over a shallow sand bar. He held me afterward. Then, as naked but not as innocent as my born day, I jumped overboard and washed it all away in the Bimini tide. The boat sped back to Whale Cay – girl turned woman on the bough.

Two days later his boss came to the island. They would go on a fishing expedition. "I will be back soon." Those words are, for me, a cherished memory because they were the last.

He was gone in two days, the people came, left, and word was they would return with big fish. That sporty boy, gold toothy smile, went everywhere with those 'Mericans; he even got their talk, but that's a Bimini boy, just styling like a big shot. I washed and kept his shirt from the laundry – my only keepsake. Well not quite – I almost had a big forgetfulness. Petunia is his!

That boy had dreams bigger than Bimini and all the islands, and, the sad thing; I still have big dreams about him. It's just that he is on the inside of mine, and I'm on the outside of his. He would have come back to Whale Cay, hell, hurricane, or high tide if I was on his mind.

Hate to admit, but my whole life spinning, watching the

Bradford boy leave my girl with that baby. Now, that's going to be my child too – and it's no never mind to me because it's five children I done brought up. The good thing is children don't leave.

Lord, I got work, and I thank you for strength. But I have a big hurting that can't stop. These secrets pain so bad.

Anyway, I got to fix dinner for Bertram and the children, but before that, let me pull up them weeds in front of the great wall in my backyard. That is life – always keep your side clean. That is me, a woman of good character and behavior, except for this one stain. I keep on asking, that I could be inside of somebody's dreams and not on the outside, not just plain left outside.

Not Mrs. Rolle

Bet returned to Daytona to normal school. Brad went to fix cars in Miami – a chance to leave farm work. They exchanged letters once. Both wrote short letters – salutary and cautious; both of them checking the waters between them, again.

In February of the new year, while she studied for first exams, she interrupted the pages of her concentration with this alarming thought: it was two months, nothing in two months. She was always regular.

Oh no! Oh God, no!

The doctor did little. He offered her congratulations, matter-of-factly, reading from the file in his grip. "Good luck, Mrs. Rolle."

Bet did not know what to think. She looked blankly at his spectacles, not bothering to correct, that she was Miss Rolle, not married.

She took four weeks to write the four-page letter to Brad. And she filled the pages telling him about the books she was learning – sharing with him her learning, which complemented his quest for knowledge. One line, however, said what he really needed to know, "I might be pregnant."

Brad read the extraordinary line on the ordinary page filled with her precise and upright letters made in blue India ink. He had not yet washed his hands. Car grease fingerprints spotted the envelope. He pushed the letter into his back pocket and went to the outside spigot to clean his hands with Tide detergent.

He tried to scrub from his mind what had happened. This was the second time. This time was the least expected. But this time was most welcomed. He was not sure, but his chest warmed with pride. Then he thought of Petunia and her baby – no, his baby. He tried to shut his mind up. He scrubbed the underside of his fingers, but the grimy grease persisted.

The next week, Sunday morning he drove straight past Palm Beach, all the way to Daytona. He told not a soul. He got there with the sun shining and the breeze blowing.

Twice he asked directions before encountering a thin-faced woman at the dormitory house where Bet lived. The woman fetched Bet, never allowing Brad into the waiting room.

Beatrice expressed nothing when she came to the door and saw him. She said, "I have to get my shoes. I'll be right back."

They sat on a bench to the side of the house. She smoothed out her skirt.

"Are you feeling all right?" he asked.

"I'm fine," she answered. "Certainly, I am surprised to see you here. I guess you got my letter."

"Yep, I got it." He looked at the persistent grime under his fingernails. "So are you... is it true?"

She smiled a sad kind of smile, as his voice trailed off, and hers picked up. "Yes, Bradford, I am about six weeks. Sorry to tell you like that, you know in the letter. But you shouldn't have come all the way up here – I'm okay, you know."

Bradford scratched the place above his knee where his pants rubbed dry skin. "I wanted to come. Now I get to see a college, up close... and I get to see you. I've been thinking about you a lot."

She rested her head into her own arms, supported by her

elbows on the backrest of the bench. "Bradford, I need to tell you something. About the baby, you know. Everything is goin' to turn out just fine. See I am grown, soon to be responsible for myself once I finish here and get a job. I know girls younger than me already raising children. Compared to them, I guess I'm starting late." Her eyes were clear-brown.

He did not expect that. He felt a breeze like a mama-blowing-dust-from-a-child's-eye. With such a fresh honesty in the air, he knew this was the time to tell her the Petunia story. To make a clean start between them. No it was not, Brad countered, hoping for a magic poof to make everything right. He looked at her, head in her own arm, soft voice in his ears. She was a little girl about to take on a brave job. Petunia accused and pouted, Beatrice accepted and smiled. And Brad wanted right then to lift her up and take her home – to Miami, no, to Nassau!

But, sitting sideways on the bench, he merely reached to touch her curled arm, but not finding enough courage to even grasp her slender, naked fingers.

She still eased out kind words. "And this is my last term. I'll be graduated from here before anyone knows…" then she interrupted herself. "Oh, but Mama and Papa will be so disappointed in me, they done sacrificed so much, and I won't be able to start teaching at Industrial High. "They might not hire me any more…" She too had conflicting moods.

With his fingers hovering, awkwardly, above her arm, she sank her head deeper into her own shoulder.

"I'm in love with you Beatrice." Where did that come from? He did not know, but he felt grateful. Grateful, that it was just the two of them, alone, without her watchful father, Ebenezer, looming about. Ebenezer liked him, and he liked Ebenezer's daughter. The old man liked young men not afraid of hard work.

Yet his gratitude made him think of swimming underwater – everything blurry. Then, out of breath, he would burst through the surface, and swallow fresh air, and blink his eyes open to the expanse of clear blue water and horizons, and to the fishing boat safely rocking in the waves. She was his ship come in, right there in front of him. So he felt and meant gratitude, but thought and said, "I'm in love."

She stretched from her slender neck – what a splendor! With her head erect, and in full beauty, she showed him wistful eyes, and said nothing.

"I want to marry you." His voice gargled, and then grew confident. "I know you care for me; I know that, but you a college girl. I never did think you would want to marry, but I know better now. You might be more educated, but you are nice, not stuck-up. We suit each other, and I am goin' to better myself, so you won't be ashamed of me."

Now the adrenaline pumped, and caution flew to the winds. Now he could grab her forbidden fingers. Thoughts of Petunia were pushed aside, or inside, and he looked at Beatrice and her flawless neck.

She looked his way again, and spoke deliberately, like the schoolteacher she planned on becoming. "I do not want you to marry me out of obligation. I know you want to do right, but if I marry a man, it got to be more than because I got his baby in my stomach. But I just don't want that. No!"

"Listen here, I never tell no woman I love her before I tell you." You the first one. You know why? For every man, there is one-woman God put there for him. You that woman, especially for me; that is the God's truth, Beatrice."

"I believe you," she spoke out of her posture. "I have feelings too, for you. Otherwise, I would not have let you… you know... I'm not that type of girl. But, facts are facts, and we have to squarely face them. I'm an American, and you will have to go back home to Nassau."

He had displaced that thought during the rush of exuberance. Good God Almighty! What about Petunia? What about Georgia?

"I can stay here and work, and we can save enough to move back home – to Nassau." He said that, but he felt like a drunkard, lying about his drinking.

"I don't know a thing about Nassau, except what Papa tell me, and he not even from Nassau, he from one of those – what you call them – Out Islands. And look at all the Nassau people coming this side to work. How will you support a family, how will you get a job; if you had to come over here to work, how are you going back there to find work. Ain't no jobs over there, Brad."

He was close to her, close enough to whiff in her perfume. She had sprinkled herself right after he showed up by surprise. "Okay, I'll stay here and work. I don't care. I just want you for me; you are the one for me. Where we live, we'll cross that bridge when we get to it."

She laughed. "You island boys like to take a chance. You just like Papa, driving my Mama crazy, taking a chance, crossing that bridge when you get there. Ya'll are crazy. But then again I reckon ya'll in my blood. I guess that's why I understand you."

He gripped her wrist. "You see, you see, God put us together." He looked into the very clear eyes of this woman, and said, "You crazy like the rest of us, the same blood as us – you just born on the other side of the water."

Brad glimpsed a glint of fire, a sparkle, in her eyes. He thought briefly, dead quick, about the girl in Nassau. "I'll deal with that matter later," he resolved.

He slipped his palms over hers and shifted his knees to the grassy ground. His smile grew magnificent, as his mouth opened slightly. "Bet do you love me enough to marry me?"

"Yes," she answered. Now the sparkle filled her eyes, and they glimmered with wetness, everything inside melting to running water. Of course, she did, what else could be stirring inside her innermost belly. She would be, not Mrs. Rolle, but Mrs. Collins.

The duck pond behind them reflected the afternoon sun, which slid from the obscurity of graying clouds. They felt the warmth of the fresh sun. Her neck relaxed. His head leaned into her body. They absorbed the new energy, and both felt the deep resonations caused by a forest of possibility.

Daddy's Gone Away

In Nassau, Petunia, Brad and the baby girl, Georgia, had ever-expanding connections through the large tube-radio, which stayed on until it signed off. The brown talking box was a gift from his parents. His daddy loved radios, being a boat captain. On the mail boat, a radio was built into the module, from where the captain steered his ship; this was in addition to the two-way radio used for emergency communication.

Walter Winchell, the famed broadcaster, used to speak directly to them, "Hello to the ships at sea." At other times, the voices of baseball broadcasters would entertain. Brad and his daddy both loved the New York Giants, and when they played the Brooklyn Dodgers chills pulsed up and down his spine. He always knew that the "Say Hey" kid would be a star, had told them so. Late Nights, Billie Holliday sang the blues, and Frank Sinatra sang love melodies in his own way. The local station was for news, and that is what the people called it – the "news station."

And that is where he got the news, after he had been 'let go' or laid off. They announced that all people wishing to sign up for contract farm work in the United States to please report to the government square beginning eight a.m. on weekdays.

Electricity pounded in Brad's body. His ears were stuck to the radio, magnetized by the nasal voice.

"I'm going to sign up for the Contract," he informed Petunia. "I should have thought about this before. I already got me a passport.

She breathed in and out, deeply in and resignedly out. "What for? I didn't know you were a farmer." She put fresh-baked loaves of bread on the wooden table to cool.

He was tying shoelaces. "All they want is people to pick fruits and vegetables. Any fool can pick an orange."

"Well, I guess me and my chile better learn to fend for ourselves. I thought you said you were going to, at least, support us. I know you wasn't goin' to marry me, cause your Ma think I ain't good enough for you. Now I just ain't goin' to be good enough, after you become an American boy, a real jazzy boy." She hung the kitchen towel, used to wipe the table, on a nail, protruding from the wall, just above a galvanized pail full of fresh water from the pump.

"I never knew a woman that could talk as much foolishness as you. In the first place, when I go over there, part of my pay will come to the government office directly for you. Just go pick it up cause your name on the contract. In the next place, just because I'm going to America don't make me better than anyone." That was his answer, but maybe he did not understand what she implied, about him not marrying her, but that was that. He felt the electricity charging his adrenaline, his mind was made up, and it didn't matter what came up in hers. His mind was on the States.

The next morning he went to sign up. The line that was not long, but it moved slowly – slowly because some of the men needed help, even to write their own names. One guy who stammered, Brad knew him from the dock, asked Brad to fill in his papers, and rewarded him with four shillings. "This is already sweet." He smiled inside.

Petunia was the one who thought up the idea of the dry goods shop. When he got paid and saved up his money in the States, she explained to him, while laying on his bold shoulders that night, how to go and buy up clothes – socks, underwear, readymade dresses, shirts, plants – and keep them in a trunk. When his stint of six months came to an end, he would bring it all back, and sell them in Nassau. He agreed, most pleasantly, because she warmed up to the idea of him going on the Contract to America.

Again, it was Petunia who heard his name called on the news. She picked out and packed up shirts, dungarees, two tailor made gabardine dress pants, all of the underwear, and that prized Ace comb.

She was the one who warmed a galvanized bucket of water on the kerosene stove and mixed it with cool water from the well to draw a warm bath for her man. While he bathed, she cracked open crab shells, extracted exquisite soft brown and flavorful crab fat, then cleaned the inner shell body. The delightful delicacy she simmered down with onions, thyme, fresh tomatoes, finally adding rice to create his favorite dish of crab and rice. "Those Americans can't cook." A busy and delightful wife. The baby, Georgia, got bathed after daddy; almost two, the cutie pie was dressed up in a white dress with a big red sash. After all were well fed and well-dressed the family walked out to Nassau Harbour. Brad carried the giant suitcase.

He remembered the time he jumped over to the other side of that giant stone wall in back of Petunia's house. His body shook now like back then, a sledgehammer pounding his heart. Climbing the hill, past the cinema, his forehead glistened, but more so Brad's eye glazed with the memory of Clark Gable filling up a magnificent screen, a lovely actress below that thinly trimmed moustache. Imaginations of smooth paved roads to come, contrasted with the potholes pitting the road they trudged, and the donkey dung little Georgia almost stepped on, except Petunia yanked her away from the mess.

Heading to Bay Street, the soon to be American daydreamed. "I will go to New York and watch Willie Mays play baseball for the Giants." That was his team, and, of course, he hated the Dodgers, except for Jackie Robinson – you got to give that to those Brooklyn Bums, they were first in letting a Negro play. Finally, at the dock, and with such accelerating excitement, he almost jumped onto the gangplank forgetting to kiss his toddler daughter and to embrace his faithful common-law wife.

He remembered, not because of a last-minute realization, but because Brad's Ma and Pa, the Guyanese Captain Collins boat captain and his Inagua wife, yelled, "Bradford!" They too came to see him off. It suddenly was both sad and pleasant.

"Stay out of trouble," said the captain who acted more like a father. "White people don't care for no colored people. Hold your tongue! Be careful."

That remark was a finger snap, which sobered Brad out of his euphoric trance, and made him prance back over the stone wall, leaving green grass and landing back among the familiar weeds of Petunia's backyard.

The stammering guy knew Captain Collins so he came over to shake hands – farewell to the older Collins and another thank you to the younger son. And with good manners, he took off his hat to the ladies.

Brad remembered to throw his daughter in the air and listen to her giggle before passing her back to the mother. He hurried through the amenities, then headed off the dock onto the deck of the ship where men were already rowdy and drunk with anticipation. "Godspeed," he heard his Mama whisper like a prayer.

In the island's tradition, men, when not working, automatically get to drinking. And "Rum and Coke" means it's time for "Rake and Scrape." And that is what greeted Brad on the boat – guitar strumming, goat-skin drumming, handsaw raking and harmonica humming. He knew the players because they all had shared drinks at Last Chance Bar. But the singer was a police officer who surprised everyone with a clear tenor – everyone cheered and encouraged. Even the Corporal was going to work for the Yankee dollar.

The engines of the ship roared. Everyone hollered. Music stopped. The sailors pulled giant ropes from the dock and secured them on the deck. The big vessel lurched away leaving foams of giant wakes and gasps of gray smoke. The band struck up another song.

What a wonderful revelry of friends, of countrymen, of family. Then why did this sudden guilt surge in his throat's hollow. "I can make it right here," he thought without thinking. "Going all the way across the water to pick some damn tomatoes don't make no sense."

Saltwater stung some of the men's eyes. Sure! The stutterer rewarded Brad again with a cold bottle. More seawater sprayed. A cool breeze from the west cooled the New World travelers and the big boat plodded forward, unhindered, to increase the chasm of blue away from land. Big and brassy Brad wiped salty moisture from his eyes.

It was Petunia that he last saw, she waved baby Georgia's hands. At last sight, the mother diminished to the baby's size, the baby to that of a baby doll. The big man's feeling bobbed like a buoy in high waters. "I made a big mistake. I belong with them."

Again the music woke up, the singer's voice refreshed by a

swish of cold beer, sang "Brown Skin Gal." The drummer, the raker, the picker and the harmonica player and many others joined with gusto. Brad did not want to hear this, instead he desired to strangle throats and throw drum, saw, guitar and harmonica overboard.

Then came his buddy with another beer. This bottle was different. It was the metaphoric corked and floating one, cast out from a distant land to drift, beyond horizons, to be never recovered or to be someday discovered on a foreign beach. And inside would be the prayer to the outside world.

People had disappeared, only tiny buildings remained on the dock, scattered houses peeped out from shoreline bushes, therefore, he looked to the people who were with him in the same boat. Some danced, some talked, all drank. His circle had widened and grown small, all at once. The world of Petunia and Georgia rested in a secret place, a perfect fit. Confidence returned: like the boy walking on a high wall, balanced and sure; like the corked bottle buoyant on the high seas, assured of its destiny; like the island boy venturing to sea, afraid but focused on a dream.

From his newfound sanctuary, he harmonized with the ex-police. His mind simultaneously reflected on Petunia and her most outstanding mark of beauty, her perfect brown complexion, and he mused how she was left behind to take care of his baby, which would be how he would always remember their romance and intimacy.

New Life

Not a soul sat during the service. Ebenezer dressed in a starched white long-sleeved shirt, without a tie. His wife was decked in domestic uniform, ready to work at the special luncheon party planned at her place of employment – the mayor's home. The couple's wedding attire were better than casual; Brad donned a sport coat and Bet wore the slim fitted dress and tight bonnet hat from last Easter. Father Patrick wore his clergy collar but minus coat or robe. The occasion would not be one to remember. These counting people don't need to measure the months between wedding and baby birth. So, the bridal party stood and repeated vows – for better or worse.

Mama Mays knew not to stay still long on Saturday morning. Knew to get her child respectably married. Talking little, she snapped everyone in place at the colored folks church for the ceremony and the photo poses quickly arranged by her cousin. Then Bet's mother pecked her newlywed daughter bye-bye and headed to arrange lunch at the Mayor's house, someone important from Tallahassee was guest of honor. All of this before Saturday noon.

Negro women finished sunset work before dawn, their houses put in order, then from day to dark arranged white women's chores and children. Nobody waits on us!

And in one day the Macon born woman conveyed such a lesson and legacy to this couple as they embarked into new life. The expedient plan would have Brad drive Beatrice, his new wife, back to school in Daytona, and return himself to Palm Beach before day's end. Mama Mays Rolle would sleep for Sunday church, while her husband Ebenezer stayed up with the light bulb for the new son to come home.

A pasture, half-dozen beef cattle, dung odor, slight breeze, expanded the entrance to Beatrice's college. The Plymouth drove the dust road past hundreds of barbed wire feet. She screwed up the passenger glass even though her neatly greased curls were well protected, a colorful kerchief around the head, neatly secured under the chin, portrayed exquisite elegance, especially with that red-hued forehead set in high royal cheekbone. The smile came when Bradford's belly growled.

"Men, always in a hurry, never admitting their needs, just wanting a woman to coax and beg them to do better." Two hours ago, she offered the fried fish and fresh bread cooked just for him, brown-paper wrapped and layered in a shoebox, still warm because of the outer newspaper covering.

"I am not hungry." Though he did swallow from the jar of lemon-squeezed juice. Then he snuggled her next to his chest, smelled Royal Crown Pomade, and politely pressed the accelerator on a full tank of gas.

"At the dorm house kitchen, I will warm it up and he will eat before going back south."

The car made it into a spacious unpaved area for parking, stopped, reversed and backed against a logged parking curb. An extremely thin woman, but it was a wiry kind of slimness, stood at the building's open door. With a smile, surely, she waved at them. Brad came around, removed his short-brimmed hat with a good day ma'am, opened up the vehicle for his bride and for her luggage, and in short order they congregated at the dormitory's entrance.

"You are Bradford, right? Congratulations. Beatrice is a splendid young woman." What a fine-tuned articulation. My, oh my!

Excited giggles gushed from inside. One smiling face came out, Beatrice's roommate. The others continued to peep, not shyly, just waiting their turn to be introduced. The lone male suddenly felt shy, embarrassed, with tightened grip on the suitcase he brought from the car. But the pleasant young woman pulled away the luggage. "I'll take that upstairs." That quick and she was gone up those broad steps, central in the entrance room.

With head bonnets covering curlers, giggles became queries. Bride Beatrice still held a shoebox of fish and bread. *How do you feel being a married woman? When will the pictures get developed?* They touched her scarf colored curls. She responded with smiles and single syllables, hoping to defer their inquiries until after the food was warmed, then he could eat, they could say goodbye and he drive back to Palm Beach. Pointing to Brad, hands upturned in a gesture of introduction, she called out his full name, and the girls gave back their own first names.

"Come and sit in this room while I go warm the fish." She gripped and guided him to a lounge of sitting chairs, two ceiling-high bookcases and one long study table with more seats. "Look around."

They followed her to the kitchen. With calf-length dresses, knee-high shorts, short-sleeved cotton blouses, these were well bred Negro women in casual attire. Excitement was in the air – the dangerous kind – and the news could not wait.

It was the Freedom Riders. Just like the Tallahassee students, a group of these women were ready to join the cause. They would board a public bus, as one body, and sit up front, not in back, and take a stand for the race, who paid the same fare as whites. It was time for change, and all over the country tides were shifting. The whole south would be challenged.

"Oh boy, we are going to get into big trouble!" Beatrice was all for the movement but this time she did not know what to think. What about the little boy, growing day by day in her womb. Suppose they club or drag us – no atrocity toward coloreds was beyond the morals of white policemen. "I cannot afford to miscarry." She envisioned the horror and it became too intense for this moment.

"Excuse me but can we talk later on about this. Let me fix Brad something to eat before he goes back home."

With hugs and pats of assurance they let her be to go light the stove fire. The gas-stove pilot light was out again so she found a matchstick, struck it against the concrete wall, watched it flame, held it to the side of the burner, and simultaneously turned on the stove. *Voom!* An explosion of bright orange was slowly adjusted to an efficient and silent blue.

She unhung the smallest of the black cast iron frying pans off the wall rack, rested it on the front burner, smeared a small slab of shortening to melt while she rescued the fish from the shoe box. It smelt like home. Her head had been hurting but not as much any more. Thick bread slices oozing with butter remained in the brown paper; these would be warmed afterward.

Brad caroused the study room, finally picking up a copy of National Geographic. On the back and inside were pictures of African tribespeople. Take away the costumed clothing, put the women in regular dresses or skirts, and the men in pants and shirts, these could be his kinfolk. He smiled. One of the pictured females, though darker complexioned, bore the full features of Beatrice, high cheeked, oval face, slender frame; it could be her auntie. He looked up and she entered the room.

"Hey, honeybunch, come look at this. These could be your relatives." No offense was meant, though he loved Bet for her light complexion, this magazine African had a darker attraction.

"Are you teasing me, Bradford? I'm no African."

"No, I'm not joking with you. Read it, right here, it says that some people from this tribe were brought to America as slaves. Maybe, this who you descend from, girl."

"Uh! I descend from Georgia on Mama side, and you know Papa from the Islands, that's why he take to you so much."

Papa Rolle would go off tangent at times and talk about the Black Star Liner and going back to Africa with some Jamaican. Mama Mays never wanted to hear. "Shush Ebenezer. Nobody wants to hear that crazy talk. Why would Americans want to go live in the jungle?"

Life was not fair, Bet mused. Brad had easily merged into the magazines and books. But he was a colored, lucky to work on a farm, and then to get a break working in a Miami mechanic shop; the world of books seemed so beyond his future.

The same with her father, he laid foundations, erected columns, poured the bell course, did the roofing and finishing touches on two homes: one he lived in, the second he rented. The second was bigger and that was her home. They knew better than bookmen. Brad could make cars and engines run, Papa could make anything out of wood; these were two smart men, and not scared to work. The heart behind her swelled chest pounded.

She called him away to follow and soon they were alone in the same grassy area by the pond as before. The heated mutton fish, only a hint of red after flour browning, was laid before him, picnic style on the bench. Bet stood, a new wife, watching in admiration and disbelief, feeding her husband for the first time.

She chattered but it was not of the nervous chitter – her mother was Mama Mays who made things happen quickly – instead it was necessary talk for needed actions. *Finals are around the corner and I would be certified to teach. I got promised a job at the new Roosevelt for coloreds. Don't worry about the baby, I got family help. You should take Papa up on the offer. A lot of people need houses fixed up, good money in that; you handy and trustworthy. We can stay home and save money for our own place. And I been thinking we should call the baby Patrick.*

Father Patrick showed them kindness – to quickly counsel and marry them. He waived the banns for them. He talked about Joseph marrying Mary without delay. Poor people are always short of time. Baby Jesus was coming and they had no time to tarry. Your precious child will be here soon – get your business in order. Yet his manner with them was patient, but he urged expediency. This guidance came from a colored cleric who believed in morality yet he knew the swift uncertainties of Negro life in the deep South, and the necessity of practicality. Bet had expected a scolding, instead she got sage advice. Patrick Collins, nice name, she inwardly smiled.

Suddenly, eruptions grumbled within. Gaseous biochemistry. Scientists attempt an explanation of what the Spirits have ordained. A being is moving inside, making room for its body within her womb. Her inside grumbles and whatever was forced out to make space suddenly spewed from her throat.

"Are you okay, baby?" Brad rested his food.

She ran toward the slight bushes to vomit what was left. He gave to her the towel place mat for the lunch picnic. Finally, after wiping as best possible, she answered. "I am all right. Mama told me about the nausea. It will go away when the baby gets bigger."

With a laugh, "I have Alka-Seltzer upstairs."

He comforted her, she assured him, holding each other with a passion neither had experienced. It was an insatiable longing for each other, but strangely they found fulfillment in the hugging and pressing. They said goodbye but somehow they welcomed something new.

A New Year with big changes, none predictable as she had imagined in her straight-forward thinking. All was planned – college, graduation, teach at the local school. Now her fears came to the fore, will he find another woman and leave me. I pray he doesn't get into trouble like so many Negro men. I had better take care of this child within me. I am not joining any Freedom Ride protest. But pride and optimism prevailed in her youthful spirit. I am going to be a mother.

Releasing his body, still holding the hands, she announced, "It's time for you to get going. You better not speed on that highway. His palms were wet with the odor of fish.

Morning's Red Sky

Clear reading spectacles graced Ebenezer Rolle's fine face. Night came and went beyond his bedtime, but he waited. The thick family bible laid on his lap. The page marker was inserted at Job; the good book was opened at the front pages set aside for recording family history.

His father, born in Exuma Island, had found the Bimini Cays and the beautiful Mary. Her long curly hair and gentle nature was enough attraction to stay and marry. These two had been transcribed top-center. The entry was made twenty years ago after Matilda announced her expectancy. And on this late night the story of storms and shipwreck and rescue and redemption looked back at him, not recorded, but memorized. Breathing deeply, he removed the glasses and rubbed burning moisture from the corner of one eye.

The tiny vessel had been overloaded with contraband cargo… Mr. Bolton overstocked the vessel. He thought they could make it over the short distance, and the crew almost did except for the high winds and overwhelming waves that caused the liquor crates to shift in the hold.

Earlier that morning the hazy red dawn stretched in the eastern sky. Young Ebenezer walked out to the wooden deck; his father was with Mr. Bolton, tall, ruddy complexioned and red-haired. His pa pointed to the sailing vessel, speaking in a deep and even voice. "Storm is brewing, sir. We have to wait until it blows over."

Mr. Bolton looked toward the approaching son, then looked back at the father. "What in tarnation are you talking about. This water is calm and clear as a mirror."

"You cannot go by appearance now. It is what goin' to happen later. All my life I have been around these seas – we gonna get some wind today. Do you feel the shift in the breeze?" The ever-gentle wind blew onto the back of Ebenezer who had reached proximity with the older men. The tone of the seaman was like a parent teaching something to a child for the first time.

The white man bristled. "I never asked your opinion. That is not what you get paid for; your job is to get this cargo across to the mainland. I have people waiting. So let's get going. Or I'll find someone else to take this load." He strode away with finality. "Make up your mind before I return." As he stepped off the short deck, father and son saw faded boot imprints in the sand.

Ebenezer returned the spectacles to its case and rose from the chair. "Where is that Bradford?" Through the window curtains he peeped into the darkness, with no response from the night. "Well, he is in God's hands." Resigning from the labor of his reflections and projections, he pulled the light bulb string hanging in the ceiling. The room disappeared from view. By instinct the father found bedroom and bed and laid beside his wife of twenty years.

Every soul who knew Mrs. Rolle well, called her Mays, the younger folk called her Mama Mays. Nothing to do with keeping a maiden name like movie actresses did, disrespectful. But her parents shortened Matilda into Mae and made her Mae Mays – a homophonic double. The Macon schoolhouse children, still not literate gave the clever nickname, all at once, two Mae's make Mays, no matter the spelling. It stuck, through childhood, adulthood, and even in marriage, to her friends, she was Mays or Mama Mays to their children. But to Ebenezer it was properly, Matilda Mays Rolle, the first name in the bible, the wife who carried and bore his firstborn.

The work old man Rolle did for Mr. Bolton was all there was, so he ventured onto the seas rather than chance the uncertainty of no income. He muttered about the foolishness of the man, about the evil of greed, which made men reckless and heartless. Then, after all the bootleg was in place, with the young son, another man named Willie, and the red-haired rum runner, they hoisted sails to head west.

On the horizon, blue skies kissed deeper hued waters. The captain expertly tacked through the channels avoiding the clear surfs of sand banks. Increasing tidal current gave the boat a steady clip. Clear sailing ahead. But behind, the tiny island was covered by fire-red haze.

Not Him

Beatrice screamed, "Not any more. I can't do this any more. I just want to get some rest."

"Push. Push." The nurse screamed in her eardrum, and urged, "Come on, honey. You've almost got it."

"Uughh. Uughh. Aaghh." Her breath exploded, deflated, body sagged, spent like a flat tube pierced by jagged stone, dulled with pain. Another exhalation as she sought to sigh. Then the contractions came back.

"Push, Bet. Your baby is coming, darling. Listen to me – take a deep breath – and when I say so, give me everything you got." This was a strangely familiar male voice, her doctor's, she heard the calm and coaxing accent, encouraging reserved fortitude from wherever.

Sweat-glazed eyebrows shadowed squinting eyelids. The blur of the physician's coverall seemed immersed in water, surrealistic. Conscious vision tried to focus on his thick moustache, which undulated and distorted in the swimming pool of Beatrice's view. With teeth revealed, she heard, "Okay, Bet. Push! Push!"

Perspiration sprayed her upper lip. Odor of female sweat, mixed with hospital phenol disinfectant, created a unique hospital essence. "Oh God. Oh God. I can't do this again. Can't do it. No. No."

"Good, Bet, good. I can see the head. We're almost there. Just a couple more pushes."

"No! I can't do any more. Please, let me rest a bit. Then I can have this baby for you. Leave me alone, now, okay."

"Push, Bet, push."

Beatrice pushed against her will. She weakly complained. Yet the friendly doctor persuaded her to try again and again. Then, suddenly, the baby slipped into his hands. She came when the new mother swore, no more, and slumped like a spent rag.

With the expertise of one who had delivered hundreds, maybe thousands, Doc clipped the navel cord. Two nurses were in the room, one veteran, in charge, another student, in training. The vet took the baby and bathed away the slime, weighed and measured the infant, squirted silver nitrate into the squinted eyes. These women did what they were taught in nursing school, and, more importantly, what was reinforced by practice, day after day, on this evening shift at the Catholic hospital in South Florida.

Every day one or another woman came, bearing babies to their ward. They delivered to these women the joy of new life, even though it was pain before pleasure. Beatrice Collins was not an exception.

"It's a baby girl," said the one in training. "Would you like to hold her?" The clock said six-thirty.

Beatrice finally relaxed her eyelids and let them close peacefully. After her consciousness had rested, as in slight meditation, she was ready, and responded. "Yes, please."

In a high-pitched feign, the young attendant sing-songed, "Want to see Mama. Here she is, this is the one who bring you here. Want her to hug you, sure you do! Yes you do." She laid the baby onto the mama's chest, covered by a cotton gown, still damp from her ordeal.

"Hi," said Bet to the tiny big-head child. She thought, "Who is this old and wrinkled looking creature. Did these people switch my baby? Well, let me just play along, don't say anything, and get more facts... I am so tired." She handed the baby back. "Can I have something to drink?" she asked.

Like Florence Nightingale, the nurse pranced away, took the baby, and returned quickly with a glass of ice cubes and water.

"Thanks," Bet sighed. It was done. First child for her man.

All of a sudden, for unknown reasons, she felt afraid, near panic. Her husband, where is he? After all, he's the one that wants a baby boy.

About one-quarter mile from the hospital, Bradford Collins poured the water chaser after Johnnie Walker Scotch, washing away the taste of raw whiskey. His bar stool was scooted close to the counter, hairy arms rested on its varnished edge with chin securely cupped in hands that had sat down the glass.

On the other side of the bar, a curly headed, dark skinned man whose open mouth displayed a gold tooth, was shrugging his shoulders. "Can't tell you what to do. Man, you gotta do what you got to do."

Bradford let out a breath. "Bet is a good woman, Charlie, but she wants to stay right here in Palm Beach with her people. Can't blame her for that. I mean to say that she should come with me to Nassau, I'm the man, but she won't fit there. That I know." His words were not yet slurred but they flowed out of the familiar warmth of intoxication in his belly.

"Just like you don't fit here," offered Charlie, silently. The bartender walked to the shelf and returned with the bottle of Johnnie Walker; it was Black, good stuff.

"You know, that's the God's honest truth. I can't take these white folks here, man. It's like every day you got to watch out for everything." His hands clutched the clear glass again to receive

Charlie's amber liquid offering. Back home we got whites too, Conchy Joe's, but they ain't half as dangerous as these ones, and they don't carry guns like them." He broadened every syllable instead of blending and blurring them, one into the other, as was the American accent.

"Well, you've got to make up your mind, amigo. My woman goes where I go. Period." Charlie was not American, but it was hard to place his way of speaking. Maybe, Trinidadian?

Across the room, like Cleopatra on her throne, sat a giant jukebox, which was silent now. On weekends, the queen sang endlessly and her patrons paid homages with coins, and hopped to her rhythm. The only other sound was a rustle of newspaper as another man in the room turned its pages. The whiskey poured like a trickle from an urn into an ornamental bathtub.

Brad wished things were as simple as the older man stated, but Charlie did not know the story hidden under the slur of liquor-talk. Alcohol is magic because it helps you forget what you can remember. The little girl, five years old. And those regrets that surfaced in dreams, he would be with them, then a tide would sweep everyone away and leave him gasping in shallow surf, not a soul in sight. He called a woman's name but could never remember the name he called.

When he came to America on the ship of contract workers they landed Brad in Miami's shipyard. A truck with make-shift benches on back carried them south to Homestead. He came to make money and send it back home. His broad muscles rippled under his singlet. The first job was harvesting grapefruits. They leaned ladders and stripped trees clean, filling endless hampers of the huge citrus fruit. This was climbing and reaching and lifting work – not easy by any means but Brad stood out because he was never lazy to work. And he had a charming good nature.

Next, he was picked by the foreman to go on the bus to North Florida, Ocala, then to the Glades. That is how he met Mister Ebenezer Rolle who needed someone to help patch his roof, which leaked over the kitchen.

Beatrice, the daughter, glimpsed his hairy chest that Saturday afternoon. Later that evening she saw more. He stayed to eat supper, cornbread, collards, catfish, peas and rice. She helped her Mama to cook and serve. She learned that Papa knew some of Brad's kin from Nassau. Well that did that – Brad was instantly transformed into family – it was something how island folk all became "Cuz," just like that. These were the waning days of her summer leave from college when he became a steady visitor and helper around their homestead. It surprised her that he was so interested in her studies, the books, why she had to go to college and learn how to teach; it was not what she expected so she gave him her interest. He had a maturity beyond appearances, and her interest evolved into intrigue. Summer ended and Beatrice returned to Daytona, having made a male friend, nothing more, during the break.

When Christmas vacation came she spent daytimes in Delray, picking beans out west, earning extra money, and Brad came out to the fields to spend precious moments with the lanky college girl whom, he discovered could fill a basket quicker than him. They sweated and laughed more freely because Papa Rolle was not around to discern the looks between them. The two drew closer together, and grew on each other during those weeks.

Bradford looked up at Charlie, saw the gold moving, and realized that their discourse had really been a pastime, not meaningful. He remembered. He raised himself from the stool, spread his fingers on the varnished bar surface, and said out loud, "I gotta get back to the hospital. What's my damage?"

"For you, it's a dollar, my friend. Congratulations!"

Brad looked over at the Queen of the Night, still dazzling even while quiet. He had swayed to her melodies, which jerked tears from grown men, and at the same time soothed their broken dreams. Like so many men he too found sweet solace in the liquor salon. Naturally, this was his refuge while she labored in the delivery room. As he erected to a full six-feet one-inch posture the naked light bulb warmed a "flat-top" haircut. From the open flap of blue jean overalls he extracted a single dollar and paid his damage before heading into the brighter outside light.

The new child rested where the nurse placed her. She was just from darkness so eyes flickered at the white light, then closed. Why had God sent her to this strange smelly place? From the pouted out lips one got no clue. Maybe, her papa who was skipping and whistling his way over had some idea. Then maybe not, after all wasn't the jauntiness in his strut and expression of expectation for a newborn son?

Across the hall Beatrice propped on a wrought iron bed drinking ice cooled water, which hardly helped her eyes shot red and lips parched white. She replaced the glass on the tiny side table. The curtain next to her bed was pulled, separating the other woman, snoring, her hospital roommate.

The shadow in the doorway loomed before the person, and then it was the student nurse's voice, and the man's voice in response. It was her man, no mistaking that accent. She heard the beat of her heart. In walked Brad. The young attendant waved and left.

"Hi, Bet. How you feeling, baby?" White teeth flashed.

"Hello, Brad." Warm feelings flooded away tiredness. Not a

thing would hurt her, ever. He would be with her forever. What would life be without him – this thought never even entered Bet's mind.

The look between them, as eyes met, was eternal longingness. Hers opened fully for the first time since the birthing. His eyebrows arched broadly like a shady tree. They held hands – something magic that lasted only a moment.

"Excuse me, but your little girl wants to see Mama and Papa." The helpful nurse stood in the doorway, white bundle in arms.

For no reason, Beatrice felt something amiss. Eternal security gave way to uneasiness creeping into her spine. Her dreamy gaze at her husband lost direction. For the life of this woman, why was she just realizing that the baby was a girl. Uncertainty overwhelmed her every will. It was a giant jigsaw puzzle, completely unsolved, except for the complete picture on the box front. Here was a daughter, in plain view, yet she sought a son. The previously red and dreamy eyes now squinted at Brad's face for disapproval. Inadequacy and anger invaded the space in back of her eye sockets.

"Want to hold your daughter?"

It took forever, or more, before the mother opened her arms and said, "Yes, please."

The bundle entangled the bed sheets, the pillows, the hospital gown, but strong slender arms secured the child. When the receiving blanket was pulled a wrinkled face peered out. The woman gazed with admiration. Without knowing or caring, Bet's eyes glistened, smoldering emotions condensed and melted in the corners. Tears bathed her coffee-with-cream colored cheekbones like new rain.

"She resembles her papa," said the nurse, as she stood and

left.

Brad heard her. What features in that wrinkled face come from him, he puzzled. The clearly opened baby brown eyes stared directly at Beatrice, deeply enmeshed with the now smiling features of the mother, immersed in the eyes that had overflowed with water. Their consciousness – new and old – at one in that moment. Isn't that how babies become old souls?

"She's been here before." Brad smiled in amazement, pulled into the magnetism of the maternal bond he observed.

Beatrice looked at his pink gums, disconnecting her attraction from the babe. She had found a relaxation, the travail of delivery forgotten, the fear of uncertainty dissipated. "I know you're right. Makes me think of Granma Constance. That's Mama's mother."

"How you mean, Bet? I was the one who drove your parents to Ocala when she was sick. You couldn't come because you were in college." Though he lived in Miami, helped out in the mechanic shop, it was not unusual to drive the US Route One for one and a half hours to Palm Beach, its curves and stop signs had become like a friend, therefore, on many a free weekend he would help out old man Ebenezer with odd jobs. He remembered the lumbering path toward North Central Florida and the home of Mama Mays mother, Constance. The wheelchair could not confine her elegance. It was her high cheeks, which Beatrice inherited, and her light complexion, tanned but not darkened, that Brad remembered.

"That's right. Mama was so pleased you did that. You know Granma is from Macon, Georgia folk. That's where Mama was raised as well. They moved to Florida after things got so bad up there."

Brad knew what "got bad" meant, as all colored folk did.

Florida was bad too, but not so terrible. Then, looking at the wizened infant, his heart dreaded her destiny as a Negro female; how could he keep her safe. "It's a shame we catch so much hell, all over this country."

"This baby gotta learn to fend for herself and fight just like a man." Bet said this slowly, thoughtfully. "With all the Negro boys being lynched, going to jail for no reason, we women don't have men around for protection. Then some colored men so drunken and lazy and go make children they won't even support with a loaf of bread." She held the newborn to her bosom.

He heard a resolve that always existed with her, for sure, but for the first time it resonated in his ear and engendered new respect. "Yes. My God, you are right. She going to be a warrior woman, like those ones in the magazine I saw at your school. Those Watusi women with the spears, fighting for freedom. Remember, I said, ya'll might be descended from them. I am serious, no kidding."

Brad looked at the newly arrived one. All possibilities opened. What could stop him from teaching her how to cast a fishing line, to load a shotgun, to fix an engine. Absolutely nothing. Memories of ancestors past flash-flooded his consciousness – these women had chopped sugar canes, rowed boats, delivered children while working in the fields, their hands calloused with bruises, yet soft enough to nurse the wounds of their babies and their men. He warmed up while the whiskey wore off.

Bet smiled, and declared with a dangerous calm, as if speaking from the center of a storm, "She's going to be a warrior and a woman. When you colored that's the only way." As she looked down, the clear brown baby eyes were once again fixated on her mother's stringy arm muscles.

Primordial

The baby began to cry, to interrupt their conversation, started raspy but throaty sounds resonated with vocal cords, became louder and urgent. The mother reacted – this is mine to raise! Oscillating sounds, octaves of bass, tenor, alto and soprano, became amplified from eternal cords of memory, and she had a listening ear, mumbling voices, Mama's rumbling stomach, and chairs scraping on the floor. It was a symphony of old and new finding harmony in a hospital room.

Gentle breeze flowed through slatted windows. Life's essence found harmony with the draft, its other, the very breath of God. They belonged together. A timeless drama in production, against a faded backdrop of women in wheelchairs, murals of Black women who had danced with spears, babies on backs, then aged to sit upon boulders with fretting hands under chins. Hovering angels directed; they were everywhere. Sound effects varied from rocking waves to the pitter-patter of rain, which chopped and splattered, dangerous and delightful, all depending whether the wind howled or hummed. And making her debut appearance, the newborn actress was rudely introduced to a hideous odor, the institution's antiseptic spray and the mother's stench.

Nine months ago she came as a beam from the setting sun, finding her space in a darkened forest with the brilliance of creation, making a memory place for all ages. This cry sustained what was remembered, what all living creatures instinctively recall, its ability to preserve an established presence. The baby was hungry and she screamed for nourishment. The mother too responded, in chorus, and let her chest and breasts become ready.

"What's the matter little mama?" asked Beatrice with a smile.

"Maybe she's hungry," Brad offered.

"I wonder if I can nurse her now." She looked for the white uniform and hat. No one in near sight. "Would you call the nurse for me, honey?"

Bradford Collins was swept into motion, two hundred pounds of flesh, muscles, ligaments, bone joined with bone, through the half-opened door, wondered the dim-lighted hallway, his stomach belched alcoholic vapors, at the end he recognized a gray-splashed hair woman speaking with whom he sought. It was Bet's mother, still dressed in the uniform of her housekeeper profession, speaking to the senior caregiver.

"Congratulations, Bradford," said mother-in-law to son-in-law. "How is my grandbaby? How is Beatrice?"

"Just fine, ma'am."

Got here soon as I could. Dinner party for the Congressman. Then I had to get home and fix supper. No time to even change clothes. Lord have mercy, my baby done had a baby. And look at you Bradford, first time father."

Brad shifted his feet, placed his hands in the high front pockets of the overalls. Her hands held a picnic basket in one and an umbrella in the other. Then with a jolt of memory he spoke to the nurse. "The baby is raising sand in the room. Must be hungry. Could you come to the room?"

"Oh, the child needs nursing. Come with me Grandma, let's go talk with our new mother."

Mama Mays turned to Brad. "You eat yet, boy? Gone on over to the house and fix yourself a plate to eat, then rest up, you hear.

Bet is going to be just fine, the baby also, I'll make sure, don't you worry none."

He nodded in obedience, savoring the aroma of fried pork chops filling the lobby from her hand basket, feeling the lining of his stomach rubbing together and growling, whiskey vapors gone leaving a dullness behind his eyelids.

As the women across the curtain woke and rustled her sheets, the baby still hollering from her lungs, Beatrice saw the two women enter the door. She said to herself, how come colored women always have to work in white clothes, even though their chores are bloody and grubby. "Hi, Mama," Bet whispered.

Mama Mays hands smelled like onion as she reached to stroke her daughter's forehead, a glancing touch. The warm fingers were clammy. They joined with the other hands to lift the crying baby, out of Beatrice's embrace, leaving an unexpected hollow. "Hush, hush, you little stinker. You mind that crying, you hear." The grandmother rocked and sang and quieted the bundle of noise.

Another woman did to her baby what she could not. Her mind went to a never before place, a floating exasperation. She grew aware of the swelling in her breast, the reason for the enlargement, and her arms were empty, without a suckling. "Give me the baby, Mama," she said in a tone underlined with sternness.

Mama Mays with a startled expression glimpse did what had been requested like a scolded child. Bet did not care, she was Mrs. Collins, not Mrs. Rolle's daughter. Imagine, this fast-handed older woman had just marched into the room and snatched her infant.

"Nurse, can I feed her?" The white hat was engaged with a task at bed's foot.

"Yes, you can, dearie. You'll need to wash yourself first. Just a minute." The lady walked quickly outside.

Mama Mays recovered in the chair, recently vacated by Brad. Her voice seemed distant. "It would be good to breast nurse that child for 12 months. Stop her from getting sick; she'll be resistant to colds. I nursed all of you way past a year. Things were different then, harder times, depression then war. Baby food was rationed. Nursed you till eighteen months, Beatrice."

A transistor radio sound came from the curtain, a sports announcer gave baseball scores. The white outfit returned with a basin of warm water and a rag, instructed her patient how to wash and how to breast-feed, encouraged her past the first discomfort and pain. Music followed the sports news. A brand new release from Billie Holiday, *Them that's got shall get. Them that's not shall lose. So the Bible said and it still is news. Mama may have, Papa may have. But God bless the child that's got his own.*

"Where did Brad go, Mama?"

"Oh, that poor fella look so tired. I sent him to the house to get something to eat. Not too much he can do here, this is women's affair." She opened the food container. "Brought something for you too, honey. Soon as you finish with the baby."

A gush of night air seeped into the room, smelt like rain though outside the gentle spray had ceased. It had cleansed what needed purging. Mama Mays felt the cool rush through thinning hair. Beatrice felt the moisture drying on her face. The baby girl ignored it all, her clicking tongue finally extracting warm fluid, which flowed down her throat, and satiated the volcanic eruptions, which had disrupted her peace.

Book 2

Patsy

Another Weeping

Patsy played on the Catholic school yard swing; and she wanted to pee when the news came; John Kennedy got shot. He was the President. She had seen him skipping rope with children, in Miami, on her Grandma's new television. That image came too her when the teaching nun gave news to the playing children, in a grave voice.

It wasn't ordinary for Sister to come out there in the playground, not at all. Tears oozed down the jaws of her aquiline face. Little Patsy stopped kicking out her legs so that the momentum of the swing slowed, the chain rope tottered like a helpless pendulum. The holy woman's hands rising from wide sleeves, garment hanging drape like, fingers beckoning to the children.

"Come around dears. This is a sad day. An evil man shot the country's leader. This is nothing but the devil's work." Her voice, unusually strained, not as normally stern.

Young fellow, snot spots above his lips, sucked, and interrupted, "Did someone shoot him with a rifle?"

"Yes it was. He was riding in a motorcade in Texas."

Patsy looked intensely at the nasally congested boy who continued, "My daddy has a rifle. When I get big, he will teach me how to shoot."

Sister's hand shot forward in retaliation, to stop his talk. "Guns are very dangerous, sonny. They are not toys. Guns kill. Do you understand?"

Nevertheless, the youth pressed. "My brother is joining the army; he will have a gun but only to kill the bad people, the communists."

"Enough! No more." With regained composure she lined up the boys and girls and headed them toward chapel, across from the grassy area. "We are all going to pray for our President."

People always praying when someone gets hurt, thought little Patsy. When her grandpa went into the hospital, that is what Grammy Mays kept telling her, Patsy you got to pray, over and over. The old lady's voice was so tearful, that is why Patsy felt that praying meant becoming weepy.

One of the bigger girls tugged Patsy, pulled her into line. The tingling of pee returned, but she obediently joined the formation. If this was Sunday school when Beatrice, her mother, taught, she would walk up and speak up, "Mama, I want to pee pee."

But Miss Bet was at weekday school, where she went after dropping off her daughter; teaching was her living job. Later, she would fetch Patsy, but before that she had to visit the sick Papa Rolle in the hospital; these days she did a lot of driving around.

Little Patricia, her real name, looked down at a clump of weedy grass, feeling the urine pressing its way out. She remembered what she did to her grandfather, such a terrible thing, just the night before, in the hospital. It was so bad. She did not mean to, but she did it, all her fault because of carelessness. Prickles pulled at the pretty white bobby socks dressing her feet. Her face flushed because she loved her grandpa so very much; how could she be so reckless?

It all began when Ebenezer was fixing the outboard motor on his boat, he tried to lift it from the stern but it slipped, fell and gashed the right foot. Bradford you should have been there to help the stubborn old man, that's what Patsy overhead from her parents. She listened to their night-time talk, especially after her mother would sometimes cry, other times raise her voice, *"how could you do this to me after I put all my trust in you,"* and Patsy would suffer the next morning because Beatrice would be red-eyed and mean-mooded. This was an attentive child.

Everyone said that luck saved his foot; only bruised, nasty cut but nothing broken was the diagnosis from the colored doctor's assistant. Just keep off the feet for a few days.

That was summertime, no school; she and her mother had been at home all the time. Months later, school started, but the foot instead of healing, became swollen and infected. Papa could not walk without limping and paining. Patsy was often asked to fetch this for grandpa – a drink of water – or that – reading glasses to read the newspaper or bible. Finally, Bradford drove him to the Miami hospital. When her daddy came back, she saw, for the first time, tears streaming down his face. Her mother cried that day also, an anguished wailing. But it was the father's red eyes, which horrified his daughter. She listened, wide awake, that night, heard her parents whisper, Papa had a tumor, cancer.

They did not tell her why grandpa had to go into the hospital, that huge, ominous gray building. Patsy knew dead people were in there. She asked the obvious, "Is Papa Rolle dead?"

Beatrice turned quickly, put down the book, closed it. "No, baby. Where did you get such an idea?" Mother embraced daughter. "Papa is going to be just fine, darling."

"But he went to the hospital. That's where dead people go, Mama." She clenched her mother's neck, her throat shoved back a fountain of tears.

"That is not true, Patricia Collins. Your grandfather is only sick. He will be in the hospital awhile, then soon he will be home again, alive, and well." Beatrice's hand warmed Patsy's back but her mother's soft chest barely shielded the girl's terror because the woman's heartbeat galloped like wild horses.

The next day, Wednesday, two days ago, Beatrice took her to the hospital, tugged Patsy into the room where Papa sat on the recliner chair, camouflaged in a white gown. The innocent child thought, ghosts always dress in white. She refused to budge from the door, pulled in the opposite direction, a tug of wills between parent and offspring. Mama won and the little one stood in front of the ghostly semblance of a man. He hobbled out of the chair to the frozen girl.

"Hello, Patsy, you behaving yourself? Come and give granddaddy a hug." White folds of the apparel spread out beyond his opened arms.

She remembered the grayish figure from the horror television show, a Boris Karloff movie, she had no business watching; it was scary. She froze because of the memory and unfroze because this apparition approached. With a bolt of instinct, her feet took off toward the open door. But another similarly clad figure entering in the path of escape. Reversing course, the collision with Papa Rolle landed the almost crippled man flat on his back.

What happened next, happened fast, she didn't remember but her behind did. Beatrice was holding her with one hand and pounding her butt with the other. "Are you trying to kill your grandfather you wicked girl, what kind of hell done got into you?"

Patsy did recollect being too scared to cry, that she was hustled out of the hospital and that she acted wild and crazy like her father. At the house, Beatrice commanded, "Go straight to bed."

But sleep would not come that night. The parent's whispers

were loud as sirens. His legs have to be amputated, that's the only chance, otherwise he will die, as sure as faith. Patsy's eyes opened wider than bedpans. Surely, the Lord would punish her; by now, she knew the figure she tackled was indeed her beloved grandfather, not a ghost, and that hospital patients were dressed in ghostly white robes.

She had injured her own, what an atrocity, and the hushed voices alarmed and affirmed the tragedy of her offence. The final judgment was obvious – it is all my fault. How do they cut off a leg? With a saw like the one in the back room? The hurting-pain causing aching and wincing from head to heel. On Judgment Day God will saw off my leg. Serves me right for being so wicked.

The teacher's voice interrupted, "The Lord will render judgment on the wicked. He was a good man and did not deserve such a fate."

Patsy hopped now because a tidal wave of urine crashed against the wall of her already expanded bladder. She joined the assembly in the chapel. They chanted Hail Mary, full of grace, then Holy Mary, mother of God. Next came Our Father who art in Heaven. Then Father spoke, the school will get all the children to make get well cards to the White House and Mrs. Kennedy. Continue to pray for the President, he concluded, and dismissed school for the day.

Outside, the older girl continued to hold her hand. Then she pointed toward the open gate. "There go your Mama. Time to go home." She left.

The Priest remained close. He had turned on a portable transistor radio and attentively listened. Beatrice entered and walked toward them in quickened pace. Patsy was completely tense. Her mother's face was now visible, reddened eyes and tear-stained cheeks. Then came the out of character screech from the

Sister, "Oh my God, he's dead."

The girl swung her head in two directions – one, to watch the Nun grope for the building wall, two, to heed her mother's call, *Patsy, Patsy.* The horror of that hospital night gripped without release. The Sister spoke again, "He was such a saintly man that the devil's agent had to kill him."

Patsy tried to clench the spot that had dammed off the pee, but she failed because her mother reached for her with that terrifying wet-faced expression associated with screaming and spanking. Knowing she was damned for her deeds, the dam in her broke. First the urine spurted like a squeezed hose, then after the little girl gave up trying to hold back, it gushed freely down her leg and into her pretty socks. Meanwhile, crying tears fell gently down the faces of the priest, the nun, and the mother.

Stories

They released Papa home, one leg amputated, a set of crutches and a swath of bandages to cover the stomp left after amputation, just below his right knee. A couple times he fell, forgetting the limb was missing, and him stubbornly refusing help. Mama Mays didn't have time to fuss with all her work responsibilities so the coaxing and getting stuff for him was left up to the children, and the one most willing to help was the penitent granddaughter, Patsy. Ever since she learned he was not dead it became her childhood mission to keep him alive and well. What a godsend for both.

In Samuel it said of Ebenezer, Hitherto hath the Lord helped. That had become the text for his life, marred by shipwreck, saved by mercy, married with family by grace, and blessed with this dutiful grandchild. Every day he turned the pages of the big bible, many days musing upon the family tree entries of the inside covers, intent on flourishing fleeting memories. The little girl listened. Her mother, who didn't have time to sit, finally bought a thick ledger book, presented it. "Papa, you should write down these memories." He did.

The leather binding was black with red trim, inside pages were lined without columns and the paper quality felt exquisitely smooth. She gave him also a fountain pen with cartridge refills; of course, he did not know how to do the replacements but Patsy, after one demonstration, took on the task, alert for when the ink writing began to fade.

Although, as much reminiscing as Ebenezer recited, he never talked about the storm. It became easier, falteringly, to write about the great wind that blew out of Hispaniola and wrecked their vessel in the Northwest Channel. Coffee crops on the island's mountain range got destroyed, but the storm was broken up, otherwise it would have wreaked terror upon the open waters. His daddy saw the black dread, thicker than clouds, approaching from the south as they navigated the last patch of green waters before the deep blue ocean chopped waves. "We need to drop anchor over there and wait out this gale," he announced. "That's our only chance. Otherwise, if we sail out on the channel, this boat would be smashed to smithereens."

Mr. Bolton remained calm, accepting. His eyes had bulged at the approaching dark bilge of clouds rising from the southern sea. The captain of the ship, an old man of the sea, dropped two anchors, sending young Ebenezer under to ensure they gripped solid rock, not sand, on the reef floor. Both anchors were secured with chain link. The cargo will keep us steady. Oh God, make haste to save us.

Will your anchor hold in the storms of life? When the clouds unfold their wings of strife? When the strong tides lift, and the cables strain, will your anchor drift, or firm remain?

Sweeter gusts of salty air had never before swept those seas, barely a ripple except for the refreshing swirls, but it was in stark contrast to the yet to be seen dark doom of southern sky. Might the Almighty suspend this experience, eternally. But though He changeth not, seasons do change and nothing lasts forever.

The boat bounced with the first sudden chop. And the weather picked up. For four hours vessel and crew plunged and swayed. Fortune came out of peril as waves filled from stern to fore adding stability to their fate, preventing capsize and disaster.

Daytime left but no stars gleamed above. Anchor chains strained but held, played tug-of-war with the solid rock. Then like a prayer answered, a pleasant breeze returned like the breath of God's calm center.

The white man slept, certainly not in religious assurance, but in eighty-proof whiskey slumber. The captain put into action the plan he had devised all along, while the American bootlegger slept. Calling the other crewman to assist, they unlatched the small dinghy and large oar, and let it down. "Get in boy, and use those oars to go that way, keep on rowing, keep on sculling. There's land to the west. Carry the boat to shallow water. The storm is traveling north and I pray God you can get out of its way before the second wind comes."

With that he gave the youth a straw basket, sewed all around, a huge purse; it contained the hard biscuits that Bahamians called heart-attack, sliced and salted sausage, cured fish, water in screw-top jars. Then, making him lift the shirt, he secured an army issued money belt around Ebenezer's abdomen. "Once you make land, get yourself some directions. There's money to pay for transport if you need it. Remember to find your way to Florida mainland and find the undertaker, ask your way to Colored Town. His name and address is in that belt. That's your kin. Now go boy. I'll find you after the storm, now go!" And, their final touch, he pressed a pocket compass in his palm.

Patsy, who had nodded off, lifted her face to see the fading writing, her alert to fetch a new cartridge. "Papa, what's that you writing?" She had learned to make out some words, but did not know the meaning. "What is s-t-o-r-m?" Her bright eyes looked up for further enlightening.

"Patsy, do you remember when your daddy nailed the boards over the windows at your house? Your mamma stayed home because school closed. Everybody stayed inside because the wind was so strong it blew down trees. That was a storm."

The inquisitive face nodded, remembering the darkness during daytime in their home. Her parents had occupied the first house Ebenezer built, now it comprised part of a compound after he constructed a second larger home, the official family residence. Patsy would spend afternoons, often until late nights with her grandparents. But during that storm she was with Brad and Beatrice in the dimness of solitude but also in the security of her nuclear family.

"That's what you writing 'bout, Papa?"

An entire two years of Ebenezer's life had been consumed with forgetting those stories; now, a doctor's diagnosis, a missing leg and two months of inactivity made his memory return. "In a way, yes, sugar." The little child's face mirrored his soul.

Remembering the clear reflection of water in the Florida Channel, a sliver of moon magnified upon the surface, which covered the depth, Patsy's grandpapa dared to face what was buried. Still no wind, but a strong current drifted them southward instead of due west. Forgetting the compass, the lad went with the flow and used the oar to steer westward when possible. This hurricane had blown out of Africa, found its way through Haiti, brushed by Cuba, and grounded their 36-foot sailing vessel on a reef in the northern Bahamas. Now the backlash, with the wind swirling in the opposite direction chased him as the storm pressed north along the Florida coast. That was godsent.

The boat bumped and swayed, and he stayed low, kept the oar in the boat; that lasted an hour, two hours, hard to gauge the duration. Ebenezer remained alert enough to rip open the basket and wet his throat with water from the jar and eat one of the hard biscuits. His body was drenched with the sea. He dozed, for how long, no telling. When his awareness returned, the compass said west-south-west, the dinghy drifted without sail, motor, or manpower. Then he saw the light, only a fleeting luminescence, but it beckoned like a lighthouse beam.

Let the lower lights be burning! Send a gleam across the wave!

Some poor struggling, fainting seaman you may rescue, you may save.

Working the oars at the stern he propelled toward darkness, knowing a light shined. An eternity passed, maybe an hour, then came familiar swishes of dashing foam, which meant shallow water. In the opposite direction, upon the horizon, gleamed a rising dawn. The boat dashed onto a beach in Marathon, one of Florida's lower keys.

Cuban fishers found the castaway, gave him hot coffee, a warm meal and dry clothes. With broken English and haltering Spanish, they surmised his situation – a storm survivor who had left others on the open sea. The crew was readymade, before he could request help, his offer of money brushed aside, not necessary. They charged up the diesel engine to cross the Florida Strait and comb the Bahama Bank for evidence or promise.

These three, two brothers and one cousin plus Ebenezer, quickly learned that laughter buoyed a heavy situation. Though, to each other, they spoke rapidly and laughed loudly, to the English speaker they slowly explained a joke's punchline, and he joined in the revelry, often not understanding, but because they guffawed from the belly.

On this clear August day, after clouds had followed the gale and the sun resumed her righteous reign of the sky, the sailors saw forever. Cool air at their back kept camaraderie pleasant, and a couple shots of dark rum made conversation flow, and allowed the young Ebenezer to divert from grief, though all eyes surveyed every shade of ocean blue.

First site was the canvas, bobbing, carried by its broken mast, a clue, then broken wooden pieces gave them direction. The top half of the vessel had been sheared off, like a barber's first cut, down to deck level. The fore was topped and dangled; only the stern remained, secured by chain and anchor. Not one soul was in sight.

Ebenezer dove underwater again, only finding a lone barracuda picking at the hull, the anchor gripping solid rock. Coming up, taking another breath, he peered into the ship's hold, only seeing casks and crates of bootleg booze. The Cubans tossed a knotted rope to secure him, under shoulders, and he went inside, this time feeling in darkness. Nothing but containers carrying intoxicating spirits.

"Grandpapa, what's the matter?" Patsy's tear-filled inquiry made him mindful of his wounded weeping, silently throbbing, flowing in rhythm with the ink oozing on the page. "Is it the storm story making you sad." His guardian angel of a granddaughter buried her plaited head in his shoulder and helped him grieve – again.

For Patsy, It's a Breeze

That moment rested in a memory place, somewhere to forget now and remember later. It would be guarded by heavenly agents, who knew the child from conception would be with her for eternity. They were there in the evening sunbeam of Florida's forest, they wafted in the wind of the bouncing sedan, which her parents rocked, and stayed with her during the breakup and get-back-together and breakup again of her parents. And when she met Wally in Tennessee, nineteen and a sophomore, there they vigilantly remained. It was hard to fathom why she would give away her innocence and muddy her luminescence, but such is freedom of choice. Guardians protect and restore, that is all.

    She met Walter outside the library of the Nashville college on a cool spring night. He wore a windbreaker with college letters printed on back. The moon perfectly reflected the sun, full and bright, floating in the cloudless night like a giant helium balloon. This girl was studious, from a family who strongly believed in and stressed education. Wally was not, but he struggled, especially in Mathematics, and feared a failing grade, so he chose to be among the serious-minded students on this enchanted evening, rather than the track meet. The thick book in his fist was very familiar.

    "Oh, you're taking Calculus. I took that class last semester." She opened the conversation, gave him a welcoming smile, after he held the exit door, and she went out front.

    "It is a total bummer, like Greek to me."

"You have to do the problems he assigns from the back of the book every night. And study the example ones from class, they are the same, except the numbers change." That was her common-sense logic.

"Well, I have to play catch-up. There's only one test, then the finals. If I don't pass them, it's my butt." Wally sounded like an eleven-year-old schoolboy though the curly moustache that danced atop his lips was assuredly that of a handsome young man. He walked her toward the campus dormitories, the girls' dorm was closest.

"If you want, I can lend you my notebook from the class."

She would bring it the following night. They stood by the side entrance to the building, her with a slight shiver despite the cardigan. He would not be at the library tomorrow, but could he arrange for another time. So Patsy did it, took her pen out and scribbled her dorm extension number on the inside cover of the Math textbook. "Call me, let me know."

Next day he did. They got to talking. Come to find out, the course in which she breezed through with an "A," he was struggling with a current "D" grade. He got his smartest idea, and asked if she had time to tutor, and offered to pay. "I'll be glad to help, no charge," she said. "We need to help each other out – that's what unity is all about."

Their first date was motivated by compassion from Patsy, desperation from Wally, and was arranged in the study hall of her female dormitory, which had less distractions than the public library. "Most of the girls stay in their rooms to study and do homework," she explained why their meeting place was most ideal.

It was straight-up work, those sessions. She showed him how to differentiate and integrate; the girl knew how to figure stuff out. However, nobody had tutored her about how players play, so when he would scoot his chair close enough to brush her knees, she never discerned that move, but continued to push him through example after example, explaining each problem to him like a grade-school teacher, and praising him like a proud parent when Wally made an "A" on the next test. The final would be comprehensive. She encouraged, "Go back through the early problems, they are easier, and you can still get a decent pass."

As he improved, she beamed. When he called her an "A+" teacher, she glowed. But Patsy was smarter than a teacher. Now, don't get it wrong, teachers are extremely smart. That is not the point; the girl wanted to become an engineer, but she settled for her mother's lot in life. But what was good enough for Beatrice limited her daughter's ambition. The Mama grew up under American Apartheid, for God's sake. In those days, yes, it was dangerous for colored women to reach too high, but this nowadays generation were changing – and changing things. Why didn't Patsy defend her choice by pointing out that the Civil Rights Act had passed?

Another matter, she knew by now to only listen to Beatrice with one ear, since whatever was said related, somehow, back to how her husband betrayed her trust in him, embarrassed her, left her single with two children, while he went back to his first family, one she never knew about before saying "I do." The mother's lone relief was to pour her emotions into the two girls and live vicariously through their life journey. Inwardly, the older daughter realized this truth, yet she went along with Bet's aspirations, cloudy as they were for a brilliant ruby like Patsy.

In any case, at the time when Wally complemented her, she was glad to be a teacher, to coach a student from "D" to "B" which would be his grade for the course. After learning he had "aced" the final, Wally called her dorm room. The roommate answered, which she often did because the calls were mostly from one of the men chasing her. Though the other woman announced that the call was for Patsy, from Walter, it was only after she had been on the phone with him for almost five minutes.

Patsy lifted her eyes from the textbook passage she had practically memorized. She uncurled lanky legs and moved from dorm bed to wall phone. "Hello," creaked from a throat that had been quiet for a spell. She cleared it.

"Hi," said he in a jovial voice. "I called to find out if you would have dinner with me tomorrow night after your exams are finished. That's when you are done, right? Just want to say, thank you."

"Yes, that's very kind of you, but I can't make it."

"Come on, you have to find time to eat. Please say yes. Dinner is the least I could do for my favorite teacher. If you like barbecue, this is the best joint in Nashville."

"You know I love it. I told you that just the other day. Not fair." A half smile escaped.

"Then that means yes."

"Okay. Okay."

"Pick you up at seven. How's that?"

"Yes. Sounds good. See you." She ended the conversation and hung up the receiver. Unexpectedly, there was a trembling in her stomach.

Returning to the text, she glanced at her roommate, they met each other's eyes briefly, before Patsy looked away. The other asked, "Are you and Wally going together? I see that you two been hanging lately."

I've been helping with his Calculus. That's all. Now he wants to take me to dinner tomorrow, which is kind of sweet. But nothing's going on. Why you ask?"

"Oh, no reason. Just curious, not minding my own beeswax." The roommate drank apple juice from her coffee cup. Where Patsy was slender, this girl had curves – the one tall and lean, the other buxom, wearing a halter tank blouse and tight shorts. The two of them got along fine.

Patsy returned to the book, but a half-hour later closed it, thinking, if I have not learned this material already, I won't learn it now. She undressed and put on pajamas, set her hair in curlers, brushed her teeth, and went to sleep.

The next night Wally picked her up in his red VW Bug. They went to the barbecue joint, shared a platter of ribs, and each pecked away at their sides, Wally had collards with cornbread, Patsy potato salad and coleslaw. When she wiped away grease and sauce, her lipstick was also smeared on the napkin. After eating and talking, drinking lemonade and laughing with one another, only bared bones remained.

She told him about her birthplace, West Palm Beach, Florida, not Palm Beach where the rich folk lived. He told her what it meant to be an "army brat," living wherever his father was stationed. However, his mother stopped the moving, petitioned for divorce, and Atlanta, Georgia became a home for him and a younger brother.

"I have a little sister, ten years younger, that follows me around and around. She wants to be grown up so badly, I tell you. She's all right though." Patsy didn't say how she felt more like a parent than a big sister, even though she couldn't fathom what being a mother meant. But Beatrice, the mother, expected so much from the eldest child. College was a welcome reprieve.

Wally laughed, and so did Patsy, at the dangerous prank he and his brother pulled, deflating the tires of a police vehicle, and running like crazy away from the diner where the cops ate free meals. "You are bad, I thought so; suppose they found out, ya'll would be in the slammer." She shook her head, an incredulous smile on her face.

He paid. She went to his apartment because there was nothing else to do, and no readymade excuse to not go; finals were done. The living room was astonishingly neat. His roommate was gone, bailed. A musty sweet fragrance permeated the place. Her naked feet, free of those platform sandals that caused her to stand equal to his height, sank into the shagged flooring. What luxury, in contrast to the girls' dorm. He went to the triple-stacked sound system, amplifier, receiver, and turntable. In diagonal corners of the room were giant speakers, which served also as table ends.

The LP Wally played was Roberta Flack's recent hit, "The First Time Ever I Saw Your Face." Patsy hummed along with the melody, accepting the reddish drink mix offered. Some island friends had introduced the Campari liqueur, gave a history of its main ingredient, a red bark that grew in the Bahamas; he thought that might be pleasing, after learning of her parents origin. The mixer was grapefruit juice. Her face screwed with the first sip, bitter, but the aftertaste, tart and sweet, relaxed her mouth into a smile. Not bad. In fact, she liked the bittersweet.

He scooted the padded footrest toward the place she sat on the couch, just in front. "You're different, you know. In a special kind of way, you really are. You don't mix with the Greek crowd, I don't see you at their parties, but you are really cool and fun to be around. I got loads of respect for you. Thanks for helping a brother out, sister."

The alcohol warmed her chest. Dinner had digested. With the pressure of exams over, she relaxed, only now realizing how she had been tensed all this term. His hand had reached for her knee.

"You are a stable kind of lady, you know, mature and all that, the kind of girl that makes a guy want to settle down."

"Hold on, hold on. Not so fast, Walter." Finally, it fathomed her that he was hitting on her. She held his hand but kept a smile on her lips.

"I am serious – as serious as a heart attack." He released her restraining fingers, got up, and went to the record player to change the vinyl album.

Patsy swallowed more of the red drink; now it went down smoothly as the ice had melted. She watched him with slanted eyes and crossed her legs on the vinyl covered sofa. He too was barefooted, his steps quiet in the lush rug. Ike Hayes made the soulful introduction, that had become a cue for every young man's rap game.

He knelt and held both of her hands. She let him. With a smile, he repeated the words of the recording, with perfect recall. The song used a play on words – the singer falling in love for the first time with this woman was akin to committing a crime for the first time – and for that he was guilty.

Vandalizing police cars is a crime, she softly laughed; her lips slightly parted. He leaned in and kissed them, a slight brush. She let him. She remembered welcoming his kisses again and again, even after they pressed upon her slender neck. As her body glided backwards, his body pressuring her into a passionate embrace, her eyes saw the blue single bulb of the lamp next to the couch. Feathers caressed her upper chest and the warmth of the drink seeped throughout her body. Her chest rose when he undid the top button of the red ruffled blouse she had adorned for their date. His after-shave lotion had a pine like fragrance. She sighed and surrendered without one plea.

He half-led, half-carried her into the bedroom, crisply cleaned like the living room. The music echoed inside.

Patsy lost her innocence in Junior High, which is another story, but this is just to say, she was no virgin. Nor had she ever been in the embrace of someone as experienced as Wally. Yet, in a way, she was; it was her first time sleeping with a man. Nor had she ever been in the embrace of someone as experienced as Wally. What he did to that girl, her head, if it had not been attached, would have flown into another dimension. That night he was the teacher. The girl got an introduction to womanly desires.

That semester the couple gave to each other a little of their best – and it made for a memorable spring. May in Tennessee can only be compared to God's Garden. Flowers of violet, orange and yellow graced the countryside outside of Nashville. Patsy drove through the blooming beauty, catching a ride with her friend back to Florida. She was as light as the breeze. It would be only a two-week break because she had already enrolled for summer classes.

Wally also would attend; he had to repeat and pass a course to stay on track for graduation. What would become of that? During the weeks, she slept often, her mind was exhausted by the pressure of constant learning. Otherwise, her time was used to drive her little sister to afterschool games, which made their mother happy. Most nights, she relaxed and ate with her grandparents, especially Papa Rolle; she had a listening ear for his anecdotes. It was not bad, but she longed to return to Tennessee.

It was good she only had two classes. Wally's place became a home away from the dormitory room. Even weeknights she found herself hanging in his crib. Her assignments were – on occasion – completed at the last moment, totally uncharacteristic Thank the Lord, through sheer brilliance; she breezed through the courses.

Their summer fling became serious; by fall, he confessed love and she put him on the phone with Mama. She returned to her academic discipline, secured and balanced by a steady boyfriend. They were chilling, just fine.

Love and learning were under management, but whenever there is peace and tranquility here comes devilish disruption and disaster. And for Patsy its advent was the *ménage à trois* gossip, an expression she had to look up in the dictionary.

Free expression was in the air, *if it feels good do it, do it if it's what you feel.* Women concerned themselves with liberation rather than chastity; high afros and short skirts were their statements. However, no respecting female wanted a reputation as a freaky-deaky.

It was a term used outside the race, not one touted about in Black parlance, and, as proof of this, the careless light-colored student who spouted the gossip was almost a cookie cutter white girl, an Oreo. She learned it, maybe among her pseudo sophisticated companions, who prided such passions worthy of an exotic phrase. But, bottom line, Black women won't share their men – at least not by choice. Oh, no!

And so it was with Wally, not completely faithful, and Patsy, absolutely dutiful, in their relationship. Here is the long and short of what led to the breakup. Read ahead if you wish but he never tried to get her to do something freaky, nothing like that. Basically, he was a player, not a pervert. But his curly hair and light brown skin made girls giggle in private. Some smiled, invitingly, at him, others flirted, boldly, making him aware of their availability, hinting at the possibilities. Without doubt, he took some up, and even followed through, with complete discretion and complicit privacy – the females had to accept that it was only on one night, or two – because he had a committed relationship.

Patsy never found out about these side affairs. She was too busy loving him and keeping up with classes, her two obsessions. Too busy for jealousy, she never listened to the well-informed dormitory grapevine, nor cultivated associates who were always in other people's business. Her time was spent in the dorm room, the classroom, and his apartment room. The roommate was Jamaican who appreciated Patsy's island roots. He looked forward to the delightful meals the Bahamian descended girl prepared for them, peas and rice, fried conch fritters, using frozen batter she brought from Florida, and the unique seasonings with which she spiced foods. But every now and then, when not cooking for them, she would eat at the college cafeteria. That is where she overheard the half-white girl utter the absurdity, *mènage á trois*.

"He must be doing both of them, now. I tell you, it's some freak action goin' on up in there." The dark-skinned gossip girl's voice level carried to Patsy's table; this was a hot piece, and she could not remain cool and calm.

She also heard the shrill laughter of the whiteish southern belle faking the French phrase. They saw her; in fact, seeing her caused them to whisper. It was about Wally. "You know he is a D-O-G, doing that Patsy and her roommate."

"Never can tell about the quiet ones, still waters on the outside, but behind closed doors they..." the high yellow one trailed on.

The truth behind their speculations was, Wally had a fling with Patsy's dorm mate, before Patsy knew either of them. The assumption was, they all were now freaking with each other. Well, that was it, the rest of the rumor, spreading like wildfire on campus grounds.

Beatrice's sweet daughter listened, heard and processed this old news slowly, overnight, letting it marinate, turning her thoughts sour, flushing bitter tears with each revelation of her ruined reputation. But those tears dried because the rumors lacked truth. Yet a paranoia flickered in her imagination, a fleeting suspicion capable of sparking deep rage. It began to feel like betrayal.

Her roommate sat quietly upon her bed when Patsy entered with only a nod and embraced the silence. Nothing was said as the space between them filled with pregnancy. Only a refrigerator hum could be heard. The girl delivered these ice-breaking words, "Everything okay, Pat?"

"Not really," said Mama Mays' granddaughter, who had a lifetime lesson in plain speaking. "Did you and Wally ever date each other?"

The girl shifted her weight. "Well, yes and no. We went out a few times but it didn't work out so I moved on. Why? What did he say?"

"He never said anything. I am just finding this out for the first time – from you. How come you never told me?"

"I thought he would tell you. Wait – girlfriend, nothing's going on between us. I hope you realize that; it never was anything worth mentioning but all of it is over. Period."

Our girl's distrusting eyes, though aimed at the bed, were not directed there; maybe toward Wally who lacked character sufficient to be open about his past affair – with her roommate; but, she, in that moment understood her mother's unhappiness, and this, unexpectedly, became her focus. Beatrice was never going to forgive her Daddy, Brad, for not revealing he had another child before they married. Patsy felt a pinch of Mama's pain in that moment. With all Wally's talk about openness and being real, he chose to keep that secret. This wretched realization began to threaten her very peace of mind.

"Patsy, I would never do something like that, you're my girl. You gotta believe me."

How can one respond when nothing comes to mind, or more precisely, when something else has grasped your conscious thoughts? Every emerging generation, as they individually mature, are shocked when it dawns upon them, they have become just like their mother, or their father. So Patsy had nothing to say to the other woman except to speak in silent body language. Her hand gesture conveyed the universal language of African-American females, flattened pushed away from her torso, which communicated several signals in one motion: never mind; this conversation is over; and I'm through with you; and Bye. Patsy walked out.

Wally came to the dorm the next evening. He held her hands and leaned into kiss his girl's lips, unaware of what had slow-boiled in her throat. She averted her face, while at the same time directly aimed her platform slippers and kicked him in the shin. He leapt back with the painful impact, instinctively raised his fist, but then thoughtfully dropped the clenched hand. "Hey, what in the hell has got into you?"

"You are the hell. Why in the devil you want to play me for a fool? And ruin my reputation,"

"What did you kick me for, woman? Have you lost your mind? What's going on, Patsy?"

"I did lose my mind, thinking you were a decent human being, but I have found it, because we are through." She stood hands akimbo, the Watusi in her close to rage.

He raised his pants and examined the raising welt. "What are you talking about? Please, let me know what the problem is?" His arms opened and stretched out from waist level.

She asked him if it was true, and he admitted, yes, but that was before her, and never after. She laid out his offense. *How come you never told? That is someone I share a room with, didn't you think it important that I know? That is so deceitful and disrespectful. You should have had the decency to tell me. Instead, I found out by accident, from a stranger. How can I trust you, ever? That's it, we are over as a couple.*

Again, after the confrontation, she walked out of her own room, causing a cross-ventilation because of the open window and the early evening breeze. Outside, where she had stormed, the slight autumn wind gently surrounded her frame, which was clad only in a tee shirt. Inside of her were warm convulsions, like bile about to choke air passages, which involuntary shook the body.

What she did not, could not know, this was ancestral trauma, Beatrice's trauma, the betrayal Black women, generation after generation, have suffered from their men folk. With all the collective tragedies pushed upon the race of African peoples, how come two young people cannot find refuge and renewal in each other's arms? She was sure her daddy dearly loved his wife, yet he lied to her, covertly by not telling her, but just as blatant and bold-faced. And if someone can pledge everlasting love to someone, yet live a double life with them, then who can be trusted? It was too much for a twenty-year old girl from Florida, though intelligent as the noon-day sun, to understand. Nevertheless, somehow she had an intuition of this generational curse, which had to be spiritually discerned because from out of the blue came the thought, I won't be like my mother. In the grassy knoll where she now sat on a green wooden bench, littered with faded brown leaves, the cool Tennessee air felt strangely warm.

Roots

Only two months ago they were a makeshift family, home away from home, Patsy, Wally, Winslow, his Jamaican roomy, all eating out of the same pot, curried chicken this night, prepared by her, along with steamed white rice and coleslaw. Winslow danced to Marley's latest jam. Patsy finished washing the dishes, left them draining, and joined the two in the living room. She pulled her fingers through shiny black curls and moved to the syncopated rhythm. A gold album lay on the floor. Wally relaxed, not dancing, but smiling and watching Winslow.

Wally poked at Winslow, who was really getting into the music. "Hey, bro, how come you Jamaicans always dancing and holding your crotch? You scared someone going to kick you there?" He laughed.

This was the kind of family fun they enjoyed. Winz, the name everyone called Winslow, quickly connected with Patsy after learning of her Island background. She knew of famous Caribbean born personalities that most Americans had never heard of, or if they did, showed no interest in. In contrast, her lover boy, Wally, was quite insular when it came to global culture. Even though he lived in other countries, it seemed his family never ventured beyond the army base and interacted with local culture. Also, Wally was not academically inclined, which was a better explanation for this apathy.

Here is a prime example. Everyone was excited about the "Roots" mini-series, all about Black people. Families sat around together and watched. The night it aired, Patsy and Winz persuaded Wally into the circle to experience history, she captured him by sitting on the rug, leaning against his knees, while he inclined on the couch. However, her electricity could not flow through his body frame, which remained passive and resistant to the shocking TV images. Were it a football or basketball game, Wally would not remain so still, but he would jump at the screen with every exciting play, and yell from the sofa.

"What is the point if Blacks descend from Africa? We are Americans now. Why live in the past?"

She realized, in that moment, this man was not socially conscious, maybe a social rebel, but intellectually, a conformist. A lifetime of indoctrination and misinformation will dull anyone's awareness unless that individual has at least a spark of curiosity to think outside of the box. "Wally, we have to know our past to understand what is happening today." She turned her head with a sad smile that hid a deeper concern.

"Truth, Sistren! A people without knowledge of their past are like trees without roots." Winz chimed in, quoting Marcus Garvey. He drank from a brown bottle of Guinness Stout.

Patsy's mind flashed back to Papa Rolle's notebook. An ocean of tears welled in her eyes. "I am grateful to my grandfather for telling me about our family history, a little bit anyway; somethings he don't like to talk about."

"He has a lot of energy for an old guy with one leg," volunteered Wally.

"Yes, he does."

"Where's he from?" asked Winz.

"The Bahamas. He left there with his daddy on a fishing boat to Florida, and they were caught in a storm. He survived but his father died at sea. He won't say much about what happened, except he washed up in one of the Florida Keys, the islands south of the mainland."

"That is interesting. Is that where you live, Key West?" queried Winz, whose family left Jamaica to settle in Brooklyn, New York; that was his microcosm, and even the source of his Jamaican identity. He knew little about the southern states, but everyone knew about Key West.

"No, I am from West Palm Beach," replied Patsy in a pensive tone. "That is where my grandparents settled. They moved there from Ocala, in the northern part of the state."

"They worked on the farms. Somehow, they ended up in Palm Beach. That's my home. Well, it is technically West Palm Beach. Palm Beach is a really an island; the millionaires live over there in their mansions."

"Mostly, the news is about rich people in Florida. Seldom do you hear about Black people. Maybe about Cubans in Miami." Wally said this, making a genuine contribution to the discourse.

Patsy looked his way, thankfully, grateful to tell her story without criticism, as a mistiness covered her brown eyes. "You want to hear something? Palm Beach Island, where all the rich people now live; that used to belong to Black people. They had farms. Papa Rolle, that's what everyone calls my grandfather, said the whites drove them off and stole the property. Now, our people are barely allowed to go over there."

"Truth! Truth! Same thing in Jamaica. One time ago, only country people lived in the hills. Now, it's the whites and Syrians living up there in dem big houses. I tell you, everywhere you go, Black people getting the wrong end of the stick." Winz was waving the empty brown bottle.

Patsy shook her head in agreement. "My grandfather bought land in the early days of West Palm Beach, a couple of lots, and he built his own house, in fact two of them, one of them is my home. He gave it to my parents, or sold it to them, something like that. I don't know. But that is where I live now, with my mother and little sister." Her daddy was gone now, but before he would be back and forth, together with his wife, then separated after a few months. He had stayed, on one occasion, over a year, long enough to help her conceive another baby girl. Now it was more than a cloud, instead a salty moisture flooded her eyes.

This was all before the careless whispers in the cafeteria had alerted her that Wally was not one to be trusted. Now she sat in the quadrangle, on the bench, under the red willow tree, which had turned to autumn red, and left residue on the ground. Her body was refreshed by the cool, and her mind revived by memories. She realized, like mother, like daughter, like it or not, the leaf does not fall far from the tree.

    Beatrice found out accidentally about the other woman, the other child; Brad left a postal money order receipt in the back pocket. Who is this Petunia? Why are you mailing $500 to Nassau? Just one doggone note, and there goes the whole family.

    Patsy no longer felt naïve. Her daddy lived life to the fullest with two families on both sides of the water. But think twice, if he had been faithful to his first common-law wife, then he would not have married her mother, and Patsy would not be, she would be blowing in the wind. Yes, it became clear as daylight, the sun would rise every morning and set every evening, without ever a shadow of Patricia Collins.

    But here she was existing, living, despite it all. Above her head were the tree's weeping but bright bloom, and below her feet, she ruminated, there were twisted roots that caused it to grow higher and higher each year.

Campari and Grapefruit Juice

Spring semester was half-finished. She got into her academic groove without the diversion of being a girlfriend and playing house on weekends. The routine to which she returned, reading ahead of the professor, completing assignments before due date, and making concerted effort to comprehend coursework, all placed her on an A-plus track.

While she focused on her work, Wally called often. Patsy just hung up on him, no time to talk. If the roomie answered, she relayed, Patsy is busy, sorry. When the roommate apologized again and again, Patsy finally explained that there was nothing to be sorry about. It was not her fault. He had failed the test of honesty and openness in a relationship, and she was getting out while the getting was good.

At the end of spring semester, she picked up her grades from the registrar's office. The Grade Point Average for this term was four point zero, Deans List. Smart lady. Her strides lengthened across concrete pavilion that marked the college's entrance, where a statue of the school's first president had been erected, a dignified bearded man. The school valued excellence, and Patricia Collins exemplified those principles. What does all of this mean? Suddenly, she turned around, answering the question before allowing it to become a conscious thought.

Walking in open sandals, dust blowing between the toes. On the far side of campus were the dormitories and she headed to the side door entrance of her building, climbed two flights of stairs to her room, and inside, she changed her garments, shedding skirt and blouse for faded red jeans and an oversized black tee shirt with a green question mark logo. Onto her shoulders, she slung the canvas bag, and exited the room and building following the same route she had entered. But this time her destination was off campus, and onto the streets of Nashville.

A broad public bus pulled up by the campus gate. She boarded. Patsy stood, even though few passengers were traveling. The vehicle lumbered along from stop to stop. A familiar Country and Western song played on the vehicle's radio. She felt the craziness about which the female singer wailed.

Day by day she had come to an understanding of her mother, this was a kind-hearted woman who trusted and loved, and learned the bitter lesson that people who absolutely adore you will still lie to you. Deceit is of the devil, sent to torture innocent souls like Beatrice. But while Patsy resisted becoming like her Mama, vulnerable and wounded, she had yet to realize the pendulum had swung – now she was becoming like the Papa, bold and reckless.

The bus stopped in front of the downtown shopping square. Her steps led to the Bottle Shop, a liquor store. In and out, she entered and returned with a brown bag. She peered into a few windows but nothing of interest was displayed. The bus came again and took her back to campus.

On this late spring evening, the sun shined bright orange in the western hills. A sudden cloud of dust disturbed her reverie; she rubbed her eyes. The rain was late this year. Dried twigs blew against the building door. She sneezed before entering. Inside of the room, it was empty and dimly lit, air ruffled the drape covering of the sash windows, and the remaining sunset was all that illuminated her residence quarter. Then she shut the window, pulled the curtain and the place became a twilight of darkness.

The lamp was flipped on. The refrigerator door was opened. She found a glass, filled it with ice cubes, then borrowed grapefruit juice from the other girl to mix with the red liqueur from the brown bag. She raised the mixture to pouted lips, braced herself for the bitterness, swished it around her tongue. A flat rectangular packet was retrieved from her dresser draw; it had come this morning. Settling her legs across the armchair, she again extracted the note and a tiny white box. The next gulp of drink tasted sweet.

The outer fold of the envelope said, "To my favorite teacher." Inside the note, she read the last line over and again. The rest of it: "Please do not sentence me to a lifetime of misery for my one mistake. I should have come clean with you from the beginning, but I was so afraid of losing you. Please forgive me for hurting you so bad. I am guilty of only one crime, and that crime is loving you. For that crime, I will gladly serve a lifetime with you."

The white box was plain. She opened it with red fingernails, sighed deeply, and dug out the slender gold ring with a single promiscuous diamond. What an exquisite piece of jewelry! Patsy let her body slump into the chair, all the air escaped her body, and she resigned herself to consider the last sentence. "Patsy, I love you dearly. Will you marry me? Wally."

Flight

American Eagle's sixteen-seater propjet veered east on approaching PBI Airport. Patsy looked through a tiny concave window onto luscious condos framed by the Palm Beach Island's green golf course. Her head felt like liquid to be swallowed from a water glass as the craft inclined, turned to circle the suburban airfield, and prepared to descend after its short gallop from Miami, sixty miles south.

Clad in blue jeans and a bulky beige sweater, which would have to be removed once the plane landed, she was ready to reach her final destination from the flight, which began in Washington, D.C. Her ten years younger baby sister had graduated from law school. Wow!

Toni Morrison's *Jazz* novel rested on her lap. Only a few pages had been read – the author's stream-of-consciousness became a maze of inky hieroglyphics, which dizzied the reader who was already unstable in the high altitude. A younger woman stealing the husband of an older woman seemed a straightforward plot, but this writer never followed such a predictable path, and this Patsy knew so she put it down for a later time.

Her light-brown fingers pressed into the airline's seat. Two popping veins bulged under a thin gold wristwatch strap. The watch was accented by a black luminous face. The black face indicated five past four; a gold strand, its second hand, swept, tirelessly, around, and around. Patsy glanced at it. The plane was plunging and bumping into thin air.

One time, at age sixteen she swam out too far from Paradise Island Beach in the Bahamas; coming back in her legs became logs. Three times Patsy tried to stand and wade, but her nose remained underwater; the fourth time her toes grasped fleeting sands, her head bobbled above surface, and her throat gagged with brine. *Thank you, Jesus!* She was on the brink of eternity.

Bradford arranged the trip as a birthday party and grand get-together between daddy and daughter. He had become quite the big shot in Nassau. By then, he and Beatrice showed no signs of ever reuniting; there was an indication, after Sylvia was born, that the two would become an American based family again, but the combination of the wife's unforgiveness and the husband's flightiness diminished any such hope. The tragedy is that her daddy lost it all by trying to have it all; the woman who bore his first child (her half-sister) would not have him back, and her mother could not know how to get him back. Destiny had sealed Bradford's fate to his real loves, good times in a bottle, and a zestful charm, which attracted both men and woman to his good nature.

It was on this visit that she met the older sister, but it was brief. The girl worked at one of the local banks and was only able to escape the teller window for a half-hour lunch. They exchanged numbers, overseas calls, and vowed to stay in contact with each other. She was pretty, a bit plump, well-dressed, and had inherited delightful brown skin from the mother, whom Patsy only saw in a wallet photograph. Patsy, a teenager, still shy, said all the right things though she was overwhelmed and lost for the words she really needed to say.

Brad's boyhood friend, a top member of the Black government, helped him to find a well-paid managerial position in a construction firm. When local Bahamians were campaigning to overthrow the white government Brad, through his buddy, left

Florida to join the movement. That was not a hard decision because Bet had found the letter and the money order, and their house was no longer a home for him. Patsy remembered the wreckage after her mother raged with shock and hurt during those tense times. That was when she found refuge and relief with her grandparents. The two never divorced. However, this was the eve of destruction for a five-year-old girl, learning for the first time to live with Daddy gone. Once again, Daddy gone and left another woman to "mind baby."

But Daddy would come back, with his characteristic bluster, bearing gifts, bringing good times, and even staying long enough to give her a baby sister, Sylvia. An observation, if you would allow, siblings are strange creatures; without the parental nucleus they can float in outer orbits of space and, sometimes, never bond. Patsy bonded with Sylvia, more through her surrogate parental role than sisterly affections, which is really why she was, at this moment, in the role of "mother," on this airplane. The truth of the matter, however, brothers and sisters bond around parent sanctioned church gatherings, barbecue picnics, Thanksgiving dinners, and even the close proximity of Mama's yells and whippings or Papa's cusses and drinking. So think about it, how could Patsy, never meeting Petunia, get to really know Petunia's daughter, Georgia – Patsy's half-sister? Therefore, that thirty-minute sandwich-shop break, between father and his two distant daughters, would have been a fair beginning for children separated by borders and waters. From here they could navigate the straits of Florida and the channels of the Bahamas.

The baby sister, Sylvia, went from high school to the University of Maryland, graduated with a bachelor's then it was law school. She got grants and student loans, but her big sister pushed every step of the way. The hooding ceremony that day belonged to Patsy as well. The two argued and fought like rivals. *You cannot wear that tight dress. You're not my mother. I know that – don't get flip with me, I am just telling you what is good.* However, semester after semester, Sylvia received neatly addressed envelopes and hand-printed notes on fancy stationary, embossed, "From the Desk of Patricia Collins" and, of course, a generous check. Patsy had a good job with the City of West Palm Beach, and, after her divorce, though a single parent, was still able to assist family.

Two months ahead of the awaited ceremony, she put in for vacation leave days to attend the ceremony, purchased round trip tickets from Palm Beach International Airport to Baltimore Washington International Airport, spent two days for the occasion and congratulatory dinner, joined by Beatrice and her male friend, and Sylvia's boyfriend; no Bradford, he was too busy, which eased the ex-wife's anxiety that she might have to make nice. Of course, the proud grandparents were not able to travel. What happened to Wally?

Well she never should have married him, all the warning signs were posted, but she deliberated and decided in the still shadows of doubt and dared to dive into a relationship with a man who chose to live in the shallow waters of life. They settled in Palm Beach. She taught high school and General Science. But it did not take more than two years for good sense to kick in. This was not for her, but for her mother, and she had matured sufficiently to metamorphosize, to become herself and leave the cocoon of Beatrice's world. She applied and was hired in the Municipal payroll department. Wally did not like her new hours because she was no longer able to pick up their infant child from daycare; he had to pitch in as his sales job allowed more flexibility. That did not turn out well. More and more the young Karen would end up with the grandparents while the daddy went out to sales calls, keeping him away from home until midnight at times. Patsy did not pay attention.

Then the girl in Miami became pregnant. She did not see that coming. They divorced within a year. She was not going to let her husband keep two families. They made very precise arrangements, Wally would pick up Karen every other weekend and pay child support; Patsy settled for an amount far less than the family court judge recommended. She made peace with the new family status and, after seven years of separation, she again became friends with her college boyfriend and ex-husband.

She enjoyed being a single mother, enjoyed success as a manager in the Finance Department at the City, where the office wall was decorated with her recently achieved Master of Public Administration diploma. Thus, with her child gone for the weekend with family friends to Disney World, it was okay to spend her thirty fifth birthday alone. This was the mindset of Patricia Collins several months ago.

The plan was to chill with music and to treat herself with pizza and wine. She used a knife to remove cellophane from the CD package of Whitney Houston's Bodyguard soundtrack and loaded the music. It played in soft stereo sound. Before she could get to the phone to order her pie, chimes sounded from the condo's door. Nobody was expected.

But the last person she could have anticipated was the one who walked in; it was Wally with a gift box, a bouquet of flowers and a slim bag containing red liqueur. His smile was as open with pleasantness as her eyes were with surprise. "Have a seat," she offered, pointing. "Somewhere. Anywhere you like."

Whitney sang in the background *Patsy empathized with the singer's plea for affection. She let down her guard, feeling suddenly safe in the presence of her ex-lover and ex-husband, and her daughter's daddy.*

Walter despised pizza so Patsy retrieved leftover rotisserie chicken from the refrigerator and quickly tossed it with vegetables and rice. They devoured the stir-fry, drank the Campari mix, and chatted as buddies, forgetting the fussing and fighting that had flawed their friendship. Walter did not try anything juvenile; what happened unfolded because it was her doing.

Smart women like Patsy know how to lock away loneliness so that it is not a bother. But when they finally, and freely, express that emotion, it is guised as a long-lost loving feeling.

Therefore, driven by mixed desires of deprivation and recklessness, that birthday night, Patsy freed her warrior. In the forest, the lioness lacks a mane, thus is not as renowned as the lion, but, unknown to many, she has the bigger bite. Wally, the player, would never realize that he had been preyed upon by an unrestrained Watusi woman.

What a huge mistake. This thought haunted conscious memory now that her feelings and desires were once again packed away in the secret place, the same recesses where dreams are laid to rest. Patsy's body shook when the plane righted itself for landing.

The runway looked like a giant architectural plan. An older white woman pointed and her husband leaned over to look out the window. Across the aisle, the young Columbian girl, traveling alone, speaking faltering English, lay her curly brown head against the seat. Patsy opened her eyelids, which she had forced shut, felt the gulp of tears and, this time refused to hold them back. She had to willfully refrain from reaching over to stroke the child. Bump! The flight had ended, but now began the long-postponed journey.

Reunion

Leaving the airport, Patsy's white Camry Toyota drove straight to her grandparent's compound in the Pleasant City neighborhood. It was time for serious discussion. Papa Rolle had purchased land in this area when the dirt was cheap, five hundred dollars for eight acres. In back of the houses were mango, citrus, and sapodilla trees; his boat on a trailer; and a shed where he kept tools and stuff.

Patsy had discerned the reason for Ebenezer's relative rich possessions. Despite being a black man in a southern town, he owned property and a boat. However, she had listened to his stories, pieced it together with what was written in his ledger journal and realized the source of his wealth.

When Ebenezer and the Cubans searched for his father in submerged waters on the Bahama Bank, they looked where he could not be found. Bodies of shipwrecked crew and rubbles of boat drifted north, toward the open ocean, destined for an uncertain providence. So the Spanish speaking men and the Bahama man took what they did find – bootlegged casks and cases of rum – a fortune once converted to cash money. It was the undertaker, whose name was committed to memory, who helped with this undercover operation. In Colored Town, it took no time to find the funeral director, who shared sympathies with the fatherless son. Then the business was handled quickly, with little need for interpretation because his father's friend spoke

Spanish. The liquor was in the boat's fish well; the boat was anchored in Biscayne Bay; that night they beached the boat and transferred its contraband cargo to coffins in back of the hearse; the money, wholesale price, exchanged hands. This mortician's business was more than dead bodies. Ebenezer split the cash with his new friends; it was more money they ever could make fishing for fish.

This money, Patsy's Papa Rolle, added to the money belt he kept close to him, and refused to spend it hoping that one day the lost daddy would show up to reclaim his possessions and his son. So he settled for two years in Homestead, worked the farm jobs, and lived off that money. *Time to move on, said the Funeral man to him one afternoon. You now in America. For the Negro man you got to keep on keeping on. There's no turning back. Bury your dead and get to living.* That is when he learned about the opportunities for coloreds in Palm Beach.

But God sees beyond our horizons, and the Creator of the expansive universe will scan the hearts of every man and woman to answer their prayers. And Zack Rolle, adrift in the Atlantic Ocean, fervently prayed, in the name of Jesus! God sent him a British freight vessel, which had been held up in Nassau because of the storm, and now its engines roared across the waves to home port.

"What is this?" said one of the crew members. He alerted the captain who saw through his binoculars the strangest of sights. It was a man enveloped by a wooden cask, floating. My God! They rescued the shipwrecked seaman, a Negro, who spoke good English, and took him to Liverpool, England.

He's got the whole world. In his hands He's got the whole wide world in His hands.

This should have been a miracle worthy of celebration for the ship's crew, but Zack was Black, not worth it to men who cared little if he lived or died; they simply followed the unwritten code, rescue a drowning man. So the boat docked, and he was abandoned to a fate in a land he had only heard about through fiction. Therefore, he followed the only path readily available, and joined the other neglected souls who traveled on the bi-ways and side alleys in the underbelly of the city. Nobody knew his name, except him.

Yet, there is always somebody for everyone, a guardian angel some say, and he found his friend. Her name was Betsy, the first genuinely poor white person he ever met. She took to him, out of curiosity, who knows, but they became partners, sharing the dregs and leftovers from those that had enough to throw away some. What is amazing about humans without choices is how quickly the body and mind adapts; and even more incredible is how we can make a new environment, even if it is cold and cold-hearted, our habitat. And Zack, a colored Bahamian with the help of Betsy, a white Englishwoman, made London his home.

The Divine mercy, which was his salvation, was not matched by human compassion; except for this flawed illiterate woman, none took pity on his plight. The depths of prejudice in those times were incomprehensible unless you experienced it firsthand. Who feels it knows. Every effort to make contact with his past was thwarted; solitary confinement behind steel doors was a fitting metaphor, except he lived in open air. He managed to write a letter but, without a return address, that effort was pointless. His only hope was prayer.

It was Betsy that brought him to the Bahamian priest. She heard his accent at the mission church's morning mass. A Black man chanting the Anglican anthems piqued her curiosity. The young Father sounded like her friend *There is a wilderness in God's mercy.*

By then Zach had contracted pneumonia. He coughed with a wretched wracking. The priest was recently graduated from seminary school, soon to return to Nassau. Of course, he knew of the Rolle family, a very common name, from Exuma, no Bimini. Zack shared his family history. The minister helped out, sent letters, found out as much as possible. The wife, Mary had died; she was a widow, the Bimini people believed at the time. No trace of the son, he was in America, somewhere, someone ventured. One of the daughters had settled in Freeport, Grand Bahama; could not find out her married name.

They met in the small office of the church rector. Zack was a shadow of the man who had survived the 1932 storm. His lungs heaved and hacked with the infection, he cried in the same tragic way. What was the point of living when you were long ago declared dead? The young priest closed his book, in which, on a few pages he had written the briefest biography of this Bahamian who drifted to Britain and was forgotten by both countries. The tragedy cut deeper – this droopy dying old man had recalled starched uniform school days when he sang with gusto and tears, *I vow to Thee My Country.* Yet, in the final days, his lone comrade was another forgotten soul, a homeless white woman who had become family.

And there's another country I've heard of long ago. Most dear to them that love her most great to them that know.

The Black cleric vowed to remember this man's saga. He would have a lifetime reminder. Later that evening, the world was shocked by the assassination of America's President John F. Kennedy. It was the last time he saw Zacchaeus Rolle alive. *Who would believe his report?*

He is despised and rejected of men; a man of sorrows, and acquainted with grief: and we hid as it were our faces from him; he was despised, and we esteemed him not... All we like sheep have gone astray; we have turned everyone to his own way; and the LORD *hath laid on him the iniquity of us all.*

Patsy used her own key to open the door to Papa Rolle and Mama Mays home. They lived alone but she would check on them, calling by phone or coming by the house. Ebenezer was snoozed in front of the television, the football game watched him. "Hey, I'm back! Where's grandma?" she asked, as his eyes fluttered open. At the same time, she peered into the kitchen, seeking signs of her the ever-active woman. "I just had the most amazing idea. Ya'll gonna love this."

"Papa, Rolle's next birthday would be number eighty." Patsy led with enthusiasm, "Let's celebrate in Nassau."

"Child, your grandfather can't travel."

"Why not," she countered. "He goes everywhere he wants. He's not an invalid." Ebenezer's cancer was healed after the amputation. "Besides, he can get to see some of his kinfolk. It's overdue. Daddy knows people that can get good hotel rates. Let's do it, grandparents. You'll work hard all your lives; time to relax and have a little fun."

The granddaughter was so excited. Grandma and Grandpa just smiled and nodded their heads.

Next would come a tougher challenge – how to persuade Beatrice. Patsy decided to make plans, then tell her mother, and give her little choice. This was about Papa Rolle, not Bet or Brad, both of them only needed to show up, out of respect and love. Patsy took charge, resolving to call her travel agent friend the next day, but, before doing that, she would make a long-distance call to her daddy tonight.

Brad fitted like a prizefighter in the Bahamas political rings. Both parties, even as they slugged it out in campaigns, had mutual respect for his unique contribution to their common cause, for which they rewarded him a nice job and a preferential lifestyle. When young Bahamians dared to make an official challenge, in 1962, against the white Bahamian government by mounting a full slate of candidates for the House of Assembly, they needed help from every corner. They got an unexpected boost from compatriots across the pond in Miami; Brad was one who joined the team. The Florida connection had already been trenched. When Bahamians hopped onto Pan-American, PanAm, from Nassau International Airport, Brad and others who took on that role, picked them up at Miami International. Sometimes, he dropped off at the downtown Hotel, which welcomed those Blacks because their money was green. Other times, he drove entire families, pregnant mothers, and wide-eyed children to their cousins in Coconut Grove. Always and inevitably, he busied an entire day with the endless shopping – from the basement of Richard's to the overstocked Cuban storefronts – these were wives and mothers who entered with a purse full of asue money and exited with bags full of merchandise to load into the airplane's cargo on the return trip.

    During the election campaign, the opposition party needed so many things, you would never imagine, from custom campaign buttons to suits for rallies. Brad had come to know the city, and the inner city. Some of the aspiring politicians recognized him from the East Street days, and from leisure times at Nassau bars. Brad showed them Florida's nightlife, a drink from Juke Joints in Dania Beach, or a lifetime opportunity to experience first class concerts at the Lyric Theatre in Overtown. While the wives shopped, he dropped off husbands to quickly say hello to stateside sweethearts. Brad helped them fulfill every desire, and he knew their secrets.

At that time, he spent a lot of time away from home in West Palm, more hours in Miami, his new marriage to Beatrice had hit a rocky path because of the postal order receipt he carelessly left unhidden. He tottered between cities, but in reality, he had become undecided about which country he wanted to live. More than likely, the storm of his wife's resentment would wane, because Black woman put up with the worst from their men, but, plain and simple, he had never decided to give up the country of his birth. Therefore, rather than fight for his marriage, he flirted, not with another woman, but with another country, and under the guise of joining a political movement, he returned to his first love, not Petunia, the other woman, but to Nassau.

He had not neglected the needs of Petunia. Not at all. His earnings from the Contract went back to her and the baby. Then from time to time he sent the money orders with money he earned working as a mechanic and helping out Ebenezer. However, after he told his mother that he was getting married, she advised, as only a mother would, "Send the money to me, Bradford. I'll make sure she gets it and uses it to take care of the child."

But what Petunia really benefited from was cloth, bolts of fabric, which Brad would buy and send back with the people who came to shop in Miami. She had discovered her talents as a seamstress and used her creativity to draw patterns of the latest gowns displayed in Sears-Roebuck and Montgomery-Ward catalog. Petunia would do well for herself as a dressmaker. In fact, she became quite the businesswoman, making baskets and hats out of straw, selling them to the tourists who came in increasing throngs to Nassau. But her staple income was school uniforms – each school required that their students wear matching colors – because this was a captive market, and a huge one. That is why she needed bolts and bolts of cotton blends.

Patsy spoke to her half-sister's mother more than once on the phone. The woman was courteous and kind to her, hoping to meet her soon, maybe when she visited again. Conversations with her sister, Georgia, ended up shorter than they should have; maybe, neither of them wanted to clear up the static on the line. It was too much for these young women to get beyond; and that is just being fair to these daughters because, in reality, it was their parents' responsibility. So the relationship remained on the surface. Petunia and Beatrice were strangers – each living on either side of Brad's duplicity – and he, evidentially, lacked the honesty to clearly communicate what these two girls turned women needed to build a bridge across the waters that separated them. So it was through Patsy's intuition that this plan was hatched.

Had Brad stayed put in Nassau, none of this would be an issue, but then God works everything according to purpose. And, beyond shadow or doubt, Bradford Collins fulfilled divine destiny by conceiving Patricia Collins in Beatrice's womb. She was on the phone, now, discussing her plans for Papa Rolle's eightieth birthday party in the Bahamas.

The celebration turned gala once the Paradise Island hotel manager offered Brad a free banquet room and discounted meals. Take care of gratuities for the servers, how about that? Great deal. Patsy paid the group travel rate, which covered hotel rooms at the luxury resort. Just pick out your outfits, Mama, and be packed when it's time to go to the airport, the daughter informed

Beatrice. Ebenezer would travel first class with his lovely wife who had spent a lifetime serving others, now it was time for her to be pampered by others. The extended clan of Rolle's from West Palm Beach arrived in Nassau, and a long white limo delivered them across the Paradise Island Bridge for an extended heavenly weekend.

An evening of dining, stretched into a night in the casino for the younger family members; for Bradford and Ebenezer, it was conversation, catching up with each other. The next day, after breakfast they toured the island, had cracked conch, peas and rice for lunch; the food had pepper; the air was hot and humid so they drank; Bahamian men flirted with the American women, told them lies, and tried to take the tourists out on a date. But that night was the banquet for Ebenezer Rolle, a born Bahamian who had become an American through a plight of nature. They would praise God the following Sunday morning, and experience church in Nassau.

After lunchtime, Georgia, picked up Patsy from the seaside restaurant. The half-sister was an encyclopedia picture of a professional. She now managed one of the bank branches, which hired her as a teller, and came directly from work. Clear blue sky molded into the ocean hue; despite a bright sun, seaside breeze blew away discomfort. "Welcome to the Bahamas," the elder sibling smiled, through bleached teeth and red lipstick.

Watching the woman maneuver the car, an unfamiliar European model, using a manual stick shift, and driving on the left-hand side kept the American on edge in the passenger seat. She pulled up beside a boutique store off the main street, and expertly parked parallel to the curb. The establishment belonged to Petunia, whom Patsy finally got to meet in person.

"Well, come here gal, and give me a hug." The first

impression of this woman was her smooth complexion, barely a forehead wrinkle, beneath a crown of silvery hair, combed back. She looked like a travel magazine illustration of someone from an exotic land. But her accent was decidedly Bahamian. "Girl, you do favor your daddy. So glad to meet you, my dear."

Before leaving the store, she had given Patsy a straw handbag, sewed her name on it in the Bahamian colors of blue, gold and black; she gave her several necklaces of coral jewelry – share them around with the other ladies, please – and, of course, enough souvenir tee shirts to go around.

"My treat," Petunia insisted. "Keep your money, chile. We is family."

Patsy asked, "Will you come to the birthday party?"

Petunia replied, "God willing, I'll be there if I can ride with Georgia."

They all hugged as a reunited family, then the sisters left.

They had one quick stop – by Petunia's mother, Georgia's grandmother, who had made coconut tart and other treats for the visitors. Her house was on the other side of town, a hectic neighborhood of busy cars sharing narrow streets with pedestrians, bikes and stray dogs. This was East Street. It was an older building but new paint had refreshed the stucco walls and the entrance way was well kept with a colorful garden of hibiscus rose, lilies and several other plants. "So, you are Bradford's daughter? You sure are a pretty thing. All the way from the United States of America."

They loaded up the sweets and hurried on to get dressed for the evening festivities. The old lady said she might join them tomorrow in church. "I can't get around nowadays like before time." She walked out with the women, stopping to pull a long weed from the path, and watched her granddaughter drive out with that Bradford's daughter.

Oh Life! She reminisced. Look how generations come and go, that's my grandbaby, driving expensive car, running the bank; just look at God work and perform wonders. That Brad gone to America and left them, just like that: I knew he was not coming back because he wouldn't have left if that was his intention. When they said he went and married the American girl it didn't upset or surprise me, not for one minute. That is what's wrong with this country, everybody want to be something foreign, something they ain't; I mean some people go to the States for a week and come back talking 'Merican. Not me, I born here and I going to stay here; this my home.

Everything done change since Brad impregnate my daughter in the outside toilet. The toilet been gone. My Petunia help me fix up this old house, add on rooms in the back, put concrete on the wooden walls, made it pretty. Everybody moving out where the white live, not me. I thank God for that girl; she took care of me after I became a widow. Bertram's liver swell up so much he looked pregnant, it wasn't long before he gone from this life. One thing about that Bradford boy, he do have a decent bone in his body, because he did send her money to raise that child.

You would think his bigshot mother would come and tell me that her son become American, and say she was sorry about how he hurt my girl child. Well, that would be like expecting to draw freshwater from the ocean. She still a pretender. Anyway, I over that; like the young people say, I moving on. Every dog has his day. Now my daughter is rich. And when that American woman kicked Brad out of the country, he came back here to be a Bahamian again. I told Petunia, if I was you, I wouldn't take him back, because he flighty; he'll leave again. But my girl ain't no fool, she already had that figured out.

Wonder what ever happened to Petunia's real daddy; never heard nothing since that day he put her inside me. Well, Bertram is her daddy, and that is that. It don't much matter any more because my generation is dying off; every week in the newspaper obituary, someone I know all my life is dead. Still, I wonder, is that Bimini boy still alive?

In the Bahamas, there is a popular thought, that you move up in society, not by what you know, but by who you know. That is not quite true, rather it is by who knows you. And Bradford Collins was known by several influential people, including the country's leader who was his childhood friend, and they stayed in touch, even after Brad moved to the States, because he visited relatives in Florida and Brad would drive him around; the two went way back. And it was the construction company Brad worked for that built the Paradise Island hotel where Ebenezer was about to celebrate the big birthday. And, because the manager knew Brad, the banquet room was stately, fit for royalty.

Ebenezer Rolle and his elegant wife were seated in king and queen fashion at the head table. Beatrice and her siblings sat at the closest round table. Patsy sat with baby sister, Sylvia, on one side, and half-sister Georgia, on the other; Petunia sat next to her daughter, secure and comfortable by the open and friendly faces of the sisters. *So you're my stepmother, said Sylvia; and that was that – relationship sealed.* Brad sat with his elderly parents, with several of Ebenezer's relatives, including the younger sister, all of whom they had found and invited to the occasion.

Ebenezer stayed in touch with his family, but only from a distance. He never returned to his native Bimini. It is strange that so many Bahamians leave home and never return, even though, in their adopted lands, they religiously preserve their home island's identity and culture; the traditional cuisine and dance, conch fritters and calypso, remains alive to this day in the Florida enclaves where Bahamian descendants reside, whether it be Key West or Fort Pierce. This was certainly the world Papa Rolle created; a home away from home. Once this homestead was established, he became a citizen of West Palm Beach, known to fellow residents as a Bahamian, and accepted as such.

Such is the true blue of America, a nation of immigrants, which has always included those from Black countries, not just ethnicities like Italians or Irish. And like others who came to America, they cook up and feed the folklore of the homeland they had come to know, and in this way, Bahamians in America have become acquainted with stories of a back-in-the-day Bahamas, when many of the matriarchs and patriarchs lived on the outer islands, rather than the reality of contemporary life in Nassau or Freeport. Therefore, Papa Rolle, a branded Bahamian in South Florida, was, practically a foreign tourist in Nassau.

And he barely recognized his own sister who had aged like him, even though he fondly remembered childhood stories from their early life on Bimini and though they had spoken every now and then – three minutes at a time – on overseas phone calls. One of those conversations happened after he learned about their mother's death. He buried his grief because he could not be in Bimini for the funeral. If you died in an Out Island your body was put in a grave the next day; there were no embalming facilities. So the two comforted each other, silently, he whispered, and she echoed, across the waters, "The Lord giveth, and the Lord taketh."

That brief eulogy caused him to reflect that he was

parentless, and to accept that he was alone from any family except his own and the one he had created in his mind and written in the forefront of a family bible. Thus, he again found a comfort, not born from resolved grief, but created out of fanciful reminiscences. He talked about the Bahamas all the time, but never physically returned.

Maybe, or possibly not, his wife had detected the depth of those unconscious thoughts. Ironically, it is so easy to hide from our most intimate companions. Maybe the man, himself, did not know what he had repressed. More, than likely, the soul that discerned his dual character, was his granddaughter who, from girlhood, had declared herself a guardian angel after his almost fatal injury and illness. Furthermore, it was Patsy who had peered between the lines of his personal ledger, and had sobbed openly with him, while the crippled man silently wept, remembering the storms he survived, but left him broken into pieces of the original man.

Brad spoke first, after the dessert of spiced rum cake with a side of ice-cream was served in gold-rimmed porcelain plates. The three-piece calypso band had rested their instruments after a medley of songs, to which the diners hummed.

He thanked each one who made it possible, remembering right down to servers and chefs. He quickly acknowledged both mothers of his children, glossing over details, avoiding embarrassment for everyone, by quickly, without pausing for reaction, recognizing his parents, the elderly Mr. and Mrs. Collins. Finally, he got to address the couple whom he referred to as his stateside parents.

Brad choked on his words, visibly moved as he remembered the man who showed him a path to maturity. It was Ebenezer that believed in his talents, and showed him how to build and restore houses. The elder man was self-taught in this field; he had watched construction projects in Miami, and studied in detail the process of building a house. The knowledge went into my head, nobody can take it out; but he shared it with Bradford. This recollection resulted in tears from a man not used to crying.

Then Mama Mays and Papa Rolle lost composure, their bodies shaking. Beatrice hastened to their table, and held her dear parents. Not a dry eye was left in the room. Brad could not finish his speech. He sat down next to his mother; she patted his shoulder. Mr. Collins, the father, rose and went to the head table, and shook Ebenezer's hand with all the sincerity he could convey in a grip, and said with a manly tone, "Thank you."

Petunia, now dubbed a stepmother to Brad's American children, reached both arms around the shoulders of Patsy and Georgia; Sylvia got up and embraced her from behind. It was nothing short of a miraculous demonstration. Petunia was moved, in another way; she looked toward Ebenezer and saw in him the father she wished she had.

Others spoke, but the words they rehearsed did not resonate, so people listened without really hearing. That is, until Ebenezer hopped up and, once his mouth opened up with words, all eyes turned on him.

"Good evening. Thank you all for such a wonderful celebration. First, let me introduce you to my heartstring. This is my wife, Matilda Mays Rolle. She's a Georgia woman, from Macon; and let me tell you, this woman don't mess around. She's the backbone of the family." Everyone cheered. Beatrice, who had stayed at the table, stood next to her father and steadied him as he stood.

"I have been through many storms in life," he continued.

"Life is not easy. But family is your anchor when those winds blow. And family is more than kinfolk, family is whoever God puts at your doorstep. What I'm saying, all of us are family."

"I love you all. Thanks so much. Now enough talking. Let the young people have some fun."

The waiters cleared tables, the people migrated from table to table, and mingled their conversations. The band returned and played its own version of the popular song, "We Are Family." Young and old danced into the night, or watched each other have a good time. Patsy danced with Petunia, rocking in unison, with her stepmother who still had moves, even though she was almost sixty years old. Magic was in the air.

Eulogy

Almighty God unto whom all hearts be open, all desires known, and from whom no secrets are hid: cleanse the thoughts of our hearts by the inspiration of thy Holy Spirit...

Service had just begun when the ushers helped Ebenezer and his party to the front row pews, roped off for them. Attending church was a birthday request, so Brad made the arrangements, and last night's dancers waltzed with him into Sunday morning church. What they experienced that day was more than a high mass, but more a divine encounter.

Mama Mays walked in front, Bet pushed the wheelchair, the other children followed, they took the front seat. Patsy and baby sister, Sylvia, sat in the second row; then they spotted Georgia coming down the aisle with her mother and grandmother, so they made room on the pew. The sisters sat side by side, three young women, newly united. Bradford had not yet arrived. Papa Rolle had attended the church of the same name in Miami's Overtown, which had taken its name from this one in Nassau's Over-the-Hill, Saint Agnes. The Miami church was founded by a Bahamian washerwoman who had been a part of the Nassau church before emigrating to Florida. The eighty-year-old man was delighted to make this pilgrimage.

Incense filled the air. The gospel was read by the deacon. It came from the fifteenth chapter of Luke, the parable of the lost son. After that another priest, not the celebrant, rose from the clergy chair and mounted the preacher's pulpit. In the Name of

Father, Son, and Holy Ghost!

"The parable of the prodigal son is a well-known bible story, which most of you all know, probably better than me," he began. "Its message is about a wayward child repenting after squandering his inheritance, and it is about a forgiving father who offers redemption to a lost child. The loving father is God, and we, all of us, who have strayed away from godly living, know that we can be restored, through God's mercy." The graying hair priest paused, reached under the pulpit desk, and lifted a notebook. "But my beloved, I want to look at this story from another angle, this morning."

"Let me ask the question. What about the unloving fathers who neglect their children, who don't care where they are in the world? What about the children who forget about fathers, and mothers, and go on living like they came into this world all by themselves? What about the parents, and the children, who fail to care about their families? Yes, let us ponder about neglectfulness and forgetfulness, this Sunday morning."

"Many years ago, while a young seminary student in England, I encountered a man who lived homeless in London. Nobody even knew his name. He barely survived, no one cared whether he lived or died. He was not from that country, but he loved its history; however, the country did not love him. They treated him like a prodigal, but, unlike the one in the bible, for him there was no hope of restoration. You see he was not always down and out, not at all."

"In fact, he was a proud man, a knowledgeable man, who had been shipwrecked by a storm, but was miraculously rescued on the high seas, and was taken by his rescuers to England. But that is all they did. They didn't try to help him find a way back home. They just left him to fend for himself among the rejected, the down and out. My friends this man was one of us; he was a Bahamian, lost in a faraway land. His native people counted him off as dead, assuming the ocean had claimed him. And we forgot about him. The lone person who cared about him was another homeless woman. She introduced me to this man, Zacchaeus Rolle."

Ebenezer shook in shock. Beatrice gasped. Patsy's mouth opened wide. Mama Mays pulled her husband's head to her bosom. The church stayed silent. God was speaking. Again the priest held up the notebook. "He asked me to help find his family. But, his wife was already dead, and I could not find any of the children. When he learned that his wife was gone, that took the life out of him. He died shortly after. But, God forgive me, I too forgot about him, and stopped looking. I too neglected him." He opened the pages of the book. "But I wrote on these pages what happened."

He climbed down from the pulpit, walked toward Ebenezer, and handed him the book. "Mr. Rolle, your father said he knew the wind would break the ship, so he sent you on that dinghy boat because he believed the tide would take you away from the wind, and toward land." Papa Rolle was weeping now, trying to stand, his daughter holding him for dear life. She took the book. He hugged the priest. Then he turned and looked in the direction of Patsy.

She too was openly in tears, so were her sisters. Petunia gazed at him; there was something very familiar about this man, she thought. Petunia's mother gasped and stared at the glint of a gold cap in his mouth. *Good God Almighty.*

An Inside Glance from Outside

Well, well, look what the wind blew back into my world. God always finishes what he started. All these years, from way back in Whale Cay, to this church in Nassau, He done bring that Bimini boy back to my presence. Soon as that preacher talked about the storm, my heart stirred up like never before; my mind reminisced back to long ago times.

Right after that American-talking Bimini boy left himself in me, then left me, saying he would go fishing, then come back to see me, the hurricane warning sounded. The men put boards on the building windows, they pulled the boats onto dryland and tied them down. That was the same 1932 storm; back then they didn't give them names like nowadays. Our boss lady said that wind came all the way from Africa to Haiti, and it was coming our way. When it came, it didn't blow down trees like we expected, it just howled like the devil.

Lord, forgive me, but I never imagined that my boy was out to sea in that gale. I was only thinking of me, myself, and I. Just like the priest told us, we are quick to neglect and forget what other people might be going through. I am thinking he left me with a baby in my belly. But the storm took him. But God saved his soul. He didn't even know about Petunia. How could he?

When Auntie found out I was missing my time of the month, she told me to marry Bertram. He was always talking nice to me, but half the time he was drunk. Back in those days you better do what those old folks said, or else. She and my mother was not about to let me ruin the family name. So I married a man who was not the father of my first-born child, that is the plain and simple truth. And Bertram knew better, he was a drunk, but not a fool.

Ah, but time is longer than rope. Only God could make everything work out for good, because I never thought my eyes would behold that gold-tooth Bimini smiling boy again. Only the Almighty can fix up things this way, can make the impossible possible.

And, to use that Bradford Collins as the fixer upper! How did he come and take up with Petunia? Then, I was so mad with him for leaving her and her baby. Boy, I was hot. Then he gone and got married to the American girl, that one sitting up there with her daddy. That one – O, great God, only you can work in such mysterious ways.

How can I tell that Beatrice lady, who Brad up and married in the States, that her sister is my Petunia, both of them daughters of one Daddy, Ebenezer Rolle?

What can I say to that elegant wife of his who I am? She is such a lady; it is obvious that he is such a gentleman because of her. You can see that she is a stern woman.

And do I tell him anything? What? That sixty years ago you left your seed in me, and it grew into that beautiful and well-dressed woman, seated over there with your grandchildren; that is my Petunia, no, our Petunia. Should I say to him that the man you have adopted as a son conceived children with both of your daughters, one in the Bahamas and the other in the States?

And Brad, where is he now? And my God, can you help me understand this conundrum, even though you used Bradford Collins to bring my baby's father back into my presence, how come you let him take so much from my Petunia – even her own father. I heard what was said – Ebenezer was like a father to me. But Petunia never got a real man, in her life, father or husband. Is that right, Lord? I know you are a just and kind God. I don't feel no kind a way about Brad, but I am only trying to understand.

Maybe, I can only tell the story to the children, the three granddaughters. They can handle the past because the past does not shame them. Yes, nowadays these young folk have a saying, I like their expression, "'Tis, what it is!" And look at that pretty thing, and she a smart one too, that Patsy, pulling everybody into one circle, bringing Petunia into the fold, doing for her what I could not do, connecting her to father's family; but no one knows this but me, and you, Lord. Is this my secret to take to the grave?

It is all in your hands, now, my blessed Savior. You control everything, the winds obey you, and your glory is brighter than the stars and the sun. I am only withering flesh, but I thank you Lord for your tender mercy, and allowing my eyes to behold what you revealed today.

My only wish is that I was not on the outside of this family, then I could tell the inside story of this family.

Epilogue

In Christ there is no east or west; these are the words of a church hymn. Nevertheless, these people who came west, from the east, have continued to distinguish themselves as westerners. Of course, as followers of Christ, this is contradictory to any doctrine of inclusion. Worse, they furthered the confusion by making distinctions between themselves – creating borders and ethnic groups. If the so-called Christians were one in Christ, there would not be such separation.

However, winds, seas, and sun do not blow, flow or shine according to human categorizations. Yet the human mind grasps at their self-created national identities, groping for meaning, rather than embracing God's natural and balanced creation, which gives Divine harmony.

The scriptures admonish mankind for not knowing where the wind comes from, or where it goes. In response, navigators have attempted to trace, name, and categorize the patterns and intensities of wind gusts. They say gusts of wind cross the Atlantic Ocean and become stronger in its warm waters. They become hurricanes and are blown north, in most instances. The meteorologists read pressure gauges, and study statistics to predict paths. But, truth, we still don't know how the wind may blow, or who may get caught up in those storms.

Yet, the answers we seek are blowing in the uncertain winds of our life. As an African historian insisted, to understand the history of people, we must study their movements, from continent to continent, from island to island, and even from neighborhood to neighborhood.

This is where we might find the substance of those stories, narrated from generation to generation. Our dreams have uniquely unfolded in the central eye of each locale – wherever we are, there we are.

By observing the drifts of human migration, we might not find out how the winds move, where they come from or where they go; but we may find out how the winds move each of us, no matter whether we live in the east or the west.

Similarly by studying religions dissertations, spending hours attempting to discern how God moves in creation, we might not discover the elusive deity; but, with a few moments of inward reflection, one can certainly experience how God moves us, whether we search in the east or the west.